bake my breath away

Twin Berry Bakery - 7

wendy meadows

Majestic Owl Publishing LLC
P.O. Box 997
Newport, NH 03773

❀ Created with Vellum

chapter one

Billy Northfield. What could Rita Knight say about the backwoods farmer she had fallen in love with and hoped to marry? What could a woman who had spent twenty years of her life being a "practical and rational" cop say about a man who tied up foulmouthed tourists who visited his farm during the Pumpkin Festival and tossed them into a corner like trapped cows?

What could a proper lady who owned a bakery with her twin sister possibly say about a man who wore overalls and a baseball cap, and owned a grumpy hound dog who didn't like the rain? What could a woman who assumed that a suit-and-tie man would end up being her Mr. Right say about a man who could solve complicated, sophisticated problems with three words while it took her all day? What could a woman who read classic literature say about a man who read *Charlie Brown* and *Marmaduke* comics…on the toilet?

Rita Knight wasn't certain what she could say about Billy Northfield as she worked through a careful and intense interrogation from her mother over the phone. "Mother, Billy is…a farmer…and he acts…like a…well, a farmer," Rita said into the kitchen telephone, feeling like a ten-tear-old trying to explain why she had stayed up past her bedtime.

Rhonda Knight, Rita's twin sister, grinned, took a sip of coffee and watched the carnival act from the kitchen table. The morning was young. Mabel Knight (aka Mother) was a very understanding woman who had a great sense of humor; however, when it came to love and romance…boy oh boy, watch out! Mabel Knight had a strict set of rules she expected her daughters to abide by. One of the rules just happened to be: date a man within your own age and mental range. In other words: no dummies.

"More coffee?" Rhonda called out, feeling comfortable in her old pink bathrobe. Rita, on the other hand, appeared very uncomfortable in the dark blue dress and high heels she had put on. Why? Rita believed that, even though Mabel Knight couldn't see her, the woman could sense if Rita was talking with her while wearing a bathrobe and bunny slippers.

Rita shot Rhonda a sharp eye. "Not funny," she said, her eyes scolding.

Rhonda grinned again, picked up a banana nut muffin (no more bran muffins since Zach had proposed to her), and tossed a wink into the air. "It's never wise to speak to Mother on an empty stomach."

"Hush," Rita whispered in a sharp tone. "What…? Oh, not you, Mother. I was telling Rhonda to stop annoying me…."

Rhonda giggled to herself and focused on her muffin. As she did, someone knocked on the back door.

"Oh, that must be the man of the hour," Rhonda exclaimed, jumping to her feet and running to the back door. "It's raining cats and dogs. I bet Billy is soaked, poor dear." Rhonda yanked open the door to a rain-soaked Billy Northfield, who was wearing a green rain jacket and holding a gray umbrella—very much resembling a sweet, silly, schoolyard boy waiting for lunch hour. "Oh, Billy," Rhonda laughed, "get in here."

"Boy howdy, these spring storms sure do like to rumble,"

Billy said in a quick voice. He threw his eyes up to the dark, stormy sky, shook his head, and then hurried into the kitchen.

Rita quickly pointed at the telephone. *"Don't talk."* Her eyes begged Billy. *"Please, not a word."*

Billy began shaking raindrops off his rain jacket and then stomped his work boots onto a pretty blue and pink back doormat that was way too girly for a farmer like himself, although Billy had to admit the little sunflowers were mighty pretty. "Who—"

"Our mother," Rhonda explained as she closed the back door. "Mother dear decided that it was time she found out Rita's intentions regarding"—Rhonda patted Billy's shoulder —"yours truly."

"Me?" Billy exclaimed.

"Who is that? I heard a man's voice!" Mabel Knight cried through the phone. "Is that Billy Northfield?"

"Oh, Billy." Rita sighed and then bowed her head. "Yes, Mother, that was Billy," she said. "Rhonda and I invited him over for breakfast while Zach is in Alabama taking care of his legal affairs."

Billy looked at Rhonda, winced, and then tiptoed over to the kitchen table like he was walking through a minefield. "I'm in trouble," he whispered.

Rita raised her head, watched Billy tiptoe over to the kitchen table, and let out a heavy breath. Why—or how—in the world had she fallen in love with a man like Billy Northfield? But for better or worse, Billy had captured her heart and the big teddy bear belonged to her. "Pour Billy a cup of coffee, okay, Rhonda?"

"You bet." Rhonda hurried over to the kitchen counter, grabbed a Charlie Brown coffee mug, filled it with piping hot coffee, and delivered it to Billy. "Your coffee, sir," she said, sounding like a waitress. "Do be careful, sir."

"You're silly." Billy grinned at Rhonda, took his coffee, and focused on Rita. Rita allowed a sweet smile to touch her eyes and then focused on her mother. Twenty minutes later she ended the call, walked over to the kitchen table, and instead of slugging Billy, gave him a gentle kiss. "Why... thanks." Billy beamed as he turned red. "What in the world was that for?"

"Oh, just for being you." Rita smiled and then decided on a cup of coffee. "Billy, my parents are anxious to meet you. Sooner or later we're going to have to plan a trip," she told him, pouring coffee into a simple blue coffee mug. Unlike Rhonda—who liked jokes and silly comics—Rita preferred a more practical style of living.

"Yep, I figured it's getting time," Billy agreed. "But we can't take a trip for the next month or so."

Rita frowned. "Why not?"

Billy raised his right hand and scratched the side of his face. "Well, you see, my cousin Benita—"

"Benita?" Rhonda interrupted and then bit down on her tongue. In her mind she saw a thin Olive Oyl–type woman covered with freckles from top to bottom and wearing a red straw dress. Oh boy...Benita. "Uh...go on, Billy."

Rita walked over to the kitchen table, sat down next to Billy, and let her hair down from the tight bun she had thrown it in. "Who is Benita, Billy?"

"Well," Billy said, scratching his face again and then making a pained face. "You see...Benita is a cousin of mine—"

"Yes, we kinda gathered that, honey," Rita told Billy, reading the man's troubled eyes.

"Yeah...I reckon you did." Billy studied his coffee, decided to take some down, and then rubbed his cheek. "Benita ain't exactly...normal...you might say."

"Oh, this is good," Rhonda said in an excited voice as thunder growled in the far distance. "Dark, rainy morning... creepy cousin...perfect."

"Well, Benita ain't exactly creepy," Billy struggled to explain. "She's more...crazy in the head."

"Crazy in the head?" Rita gulped.

"Crazier than a chicken telling jokes to a room full of wolves." Billy nodded. "Been crazy ever since she was knee high to a toad frog. My momma said she was dropped on her head. My daddy said she was just born nuts. I think it's a mixture of the two."

"Uh...Billy, honey, why exactly is this woman coming to stay with you for a month?" Rita dared to ask, feeling her heart fill with dread.

"Yes, do tell." Rhonda beamed as she rubbed her hands together. "Do tell why Cousin Benita is coming for a visit."

Billy looked into Rita's eyes and then made a face as if someone had set him on fire. "Cause...she ain't got no other place to go."

"And why is that?" Rita inquired in a hesitant voice.

"Because her acting career...let's just say Los Angeles wasn't kind to her," Billy explained and then quickly dropped his eyes. "First it was singing...then she wanted to be an astronaut...then she wanted to run for president...all kinds of crazy stuff." Billy shook his head. "This here acting stunt was the latest mess Benita got herself into."

"President?" Rhonda asked and then burst out laughing. "Did your cousin really try to run for president?"

Billy popped his head up. "She sure enough did," he exclaimed. "Met a bunch of people crazier than she was out there in California—the land of the crazies if you ask me—who helped her. Woman actually got...if I recall correctly...sixteen votes."

Rhonda nearly spit out her coffee. "Sixteen votes...." She burst out laughing.

"Oh my," Rita moaned, nearly smacking her head. She looked at Billy with desperate eyes. "Billy...send this woman somewhere else...please."

"Benita ain't got no place to go," Billy explained. "Those so-called friends of hers kicked her out of their house yesterday—at least that's what I was told. Anyways, I…sent her bus fare money."

"And you're just telling me this now?" Rita asked.

"Well," Billy struggled to defend himself, "you were busy with your folks and all. It didn't seem like the proper time. Besides, I'm telling you now."

Rita put down her coffee and examined Billy's eyes. Something told Rita her husband-to-be had an ulterior motive. Why had Billy simply come right out and announced that his cousin Benita was arriving for a month-long visit? Then it hit her: Mother. "Billy Northfield…why, you sneaky skunk!" she gasped. "You knew I was planning to take you to meet my parents sometime this month!"

"What?" Rhonda asked. She looked into Rita's accusing eyes and then understood. "Oh…," she said, locking her eyes on Billy's guilty face, and then grinned. "Why, you are sneaky."

"Now hold on a minute," Billy begged. "It ain't my fault that Benita just happened to call around the same time you were planning for me to go meet your folks."

"You could have sent your cousin money for a place to stay," Rita pointed out.

"Yeah…but…." Billy nervously licked his lips. "Look, girls, Benita ain't got sense enough to handle a dollar without losing ninety-nine pennies, okay? Besides, she seemed awful upset and…well, sometimes family needs family."

"Very convenient," Rita said.

Billy quickly took a sip of his coffee. "Look, girls…Chester likes Benita and would have bitten my leg off if I would have refused to help the woman."

"Don't pass off the blame onto your poor dog," Rita griped, struggling to fight back a grin. Billy had carried out a sneaky attack…Billy, of all people. If it had been anyone else besides Billy, Rita would have been upset...but Billy...was so sweet and innocent.

"I...look, family needs family, okay?" Billy struggled to stand strong, even though he felt his legs crumbling.

Rita rolled her eyes. "Billy, you're impossible," she said and then allowed a sweet giggle to slip from her mouth. "And very sneaky...but...in a way, I suppose I should be very grateful."

"Huh?" Billy asked, his eyes widening in shock.

Rita took a sip of her coffee. "I'm not...exactly...ready for you to meet my parents, Billy," she explained and looked at Rhonda for help. "You see, my mother is...funny, charming, and very sweet...but—"

"When it comes to love, she turns into a monster," Rhonda stated simply. "The man Rita or I bring home has to pass Mabel Knight's 'inspection.'"

"Inspection?" Billy gulped.

Rita nodded. "And our daddy...well, he's...not funny. As a matter of fact, he's bland, boring, and at times...a little rude."

"When it comes to love, Matthew Knight is a block of wood," Rhonda added. "Our daddy wouldn't know romance if our mother appeared before him dressed like a giant heart. All our daddy would say is 'When's dinner?'"

"Also," Rita added in a worried voice, "our daddy can only talk to people who agree with his views on life. If someone disagrees with even one of his views, war breaks out."

"Uh...what are your daddy's views?" Billy dared to ask.

"Well," Rita gulped, "one of his views is that...a man should always wear a suit and a tie and work...in an office."

Billy glanced down at his rain jacket and work boots. "Uh...I don't wear a suit and tie...and I don't work in no office. I'm a farmer."

Rita winced. "I know, honey, which is why I suppose I

should be grateful, but…Benita?" Rita asked in a stricken voice. "Billy…any delay would be appreciated, but your cousin sounds like—"

"Trouble…yeah, I know," Billy sighed. "Benita doesn't have all of her marbles in one bag, let's just say that. But," Billy added in a caring voice, "even though Benita is…nuts… she does have a sweet heart beating inside of her soul. That woman would give you every bite of food on her plate if you asked her to. And she's honest too, sometimes…too honest. I reckon when she asked if she could come stay with me for a bit, I felt sorry for her. You see, Benita didn't have a lot of friends growing up around these parts, and I wasn't exactly a leech on her leg. Benita mostly kept to herself, did crazy things. Things that made other kids laugh at her for." Billy shook his head. "She's just a lost puppy that needs patted on the head sometimes…and this just so happens to be one of those times."

Rita glanced at Rhonda, who shrugged. "Benita is going to be your family," she told Rita and grinned.

Rita rolled her eyes. "You know, Rhonda, one of these days I'm going to sew your mouth shut with cayenne pepper."

"Spicy sewing thread…my favorite," Rhonda teased and then nodded at Billy. "Want a muffin?"

"Well, I sure am hungry," Billy admitted. "I reckon a muffin will hold me over until we get to the diner."

"And speaking of the diner," Rita fussed at Rhonda, "you need to go get dressed."

"Oh, I was kinda thinking you and Billy could have a romantic breakfast alone," Rhonda explained and then popped to her legs, startling Rita. "Just kidding…I'll be back in a flash."

Billy watched Rhonda run out of the kitchen wearing her bunny slippers and shook his head. "You two sure are opposites," he declared. "You can barely tell the two of you apart, but boy, your mouths sure aren't hard to tell apart."

"My sister is a nut," Rita informed Billy. "Maybe she was dropped on her head too."

"Nah," Billy said, smiling, "Rhonda just has a good way about her that's…free."

"And I don't?" Rita asked.

Billy winced. "No…what I meant to say was…uh…you have a good way about you too…I…." Billy made a painful face. "I…Rhonda is…funny and you…you're—"

"Not funny?" Rita snapped her arms together, watching Billy sinking in a pot of boiling water.

"No…you're funny…at times."

"At times?" Rita asked and gave Billy the eye.

Billy nearly let out a scream and almost wet his pants. No man could withstand the eye. "Uh…I think I'll go warm up the truck," he exclaimed. He jumped to his feet and ran out into the storm. Rita waited until Billy was gone and then burst out laughing. Yes, she could be funny at times—in her own way.

Benita Cayberry walked into Billy's farmhouse kitchen wearing a pink, blue, orange, and red dress that matched her pink and blue frizzy hair. The sight of the woman caused Rita's and Rhonda's jaws to hit the floor. "Morning, Cousin Billy," Benita said in a thick hillbilly drawl.

"Morning," Billy replied and threw Rita and Rhonda an eye that said, *"Please watch your tongues."* "Uh…sleep good?"

"Like a cat in a patch of catnip," Benita promised Billy and then patted a belly that was flat and hungry. The woman, at least to Rita and Rhonda, really did resemble a silly type of Olive Oyl. Benita was tall, thin, and looked starved. "What's for breakfast?"

"Coffee is on the counter," Billy explained, sitting at a warm, round kitchen table with Rita and Rhonda. Both women wore modest dresses. Rita had on a white and pink dress and Rhonda was decked out in a simple but nice yellowish brown dress. Billy, who was used to how the sisters dressed, had to give his poor eyes a minute to adjust to Benita's...uh...unique style. "Thought we could eat at the diner this morning."

"Oh, a diner." Benita smiled, hurried to fix herself a cup of coffee, grabbed four bananas out of the fruit basket, and plopped down at the kitchen table next to Billy. "I just love diners."

Rita watched Benita take a sip of coffee and then tear into the bananas as if she were eating her last meal. "Uh...I'm Rita Knight, by the way, and this is my sister, Rhonda Knight."

"Glad to meet you," Benita said as she shoved a banana into her mouth. "Cousin Billy told me about you. Figured it was you two gals my eyes were seeing." Benita looked at Rita and then threw her eyes at Rhonda. "Crow's feet," she said, "need to use some cream...the both of you."

Billy winced. Rhonda grinned. Rita frowned. "I do not have crow's feet."

"You do too," Benita insisted, "and so does your sister... plain as day."

"I beg to differ." Rita's cheeks turned red. "I take very good care of my skin. I use a special moisturizer and—"

"Baking soda and lemon juice, every night before bed," Benita popped off. "Cheap and effective. Stop wasting your time with all that expensive junk."

Rhonda nudged Rita with her elbow. "Hey, it might be worth a shot," she teased. "We might want to try it before we turn into a couple of crows."

Rita stared at Benita. Billy had warned them that the woman was brutally honest and outspoken. "I will continue using the moisturizer of my choice, if you please."

"Say," Billy jumped in, "weather is still rough. These spring storms are going to be around for at least another week or so. It's sure flooding in Nebraska and other states up that way." Billy rubbed his neck and continued speaking. "I was thinking maybe after breakfast I'd take you two ladies home and come back to the farm and start working on some chores. Benita, you can help me."

"Rhonda and I are spending the day at the bakery," Rita informed Billy in a tone she forced to appear calm and intelligent. The woman was in no mood to lose her cool over a forty-two-year-old woman who dressed and looked like a clown.

"Lots of baking today, you know," Rhonda added, attempting to take the edge off.

"More like lots of taxes," Rita corrected Rhonda. "The tax software we used this year failed miserably. Although we ended up managing to get new software and remain in the green, we have decided to spend the next week making sure we understand the new software in order to avoid any unnecessary problems next tax season."

"And do some baking." Rhonda winked at Benita. Benita winked back.

Billy sighed. Whenever Rita dropped into one of her "practical" tones, that meant she was upset and deeply bothered. "Yeah, taxes are rough," he said. "I have a tax person do the family taxes...same person has been doing the family taxes since before Daddy went off to Heaven."

"You talking about Old Man Barney?" Benita asked.

"Sure am."

Benita wrinkled her nose. "He sure is a stuffy old fart, ain't he? Always smelled funny," she said. "Does he still smell like mothballs?"

"Well...kinda." Billy slightly nodded his head. "His office still smells like mothballs and—" Billy looked at Rita. Rita frowned. "Uh...nice man...yes sir, Old Man Barney...uh... Barney...real nice fella...decent sort, yes sir."

"In other words," Rhonda told Benita, "Billy can't say the guy farts in public as long as my sister is sitting here. She's the sophisticated kind."

"I don't believe in talking cruel words about someone when that person is not present to defend him or herself," Rita snapped at Rhonda. "I believe in manners."

"Manners is one thing," Benita told Rita, digging into a second banana, "and smelling like mothballs is another." Benita swallowed a bit of the banana. "Take me, for example. I'm a freak...and I know I'm a freak. People from all over point at me and laugh. Don't mean a thing in the world...just words. You see, inside I'm as tough as nails."

"Yes...well...that may be true, Ms. Cayberry," Rita said in a calm tone, "but I still stand by my opinion that it is rude to speak about a person when he or she is not present."

"Oh," Benita waved her hand at Rita, "we kids have been talking about Old Man Barney since we were knee high to a toad frog. That old fart don't care what we say about him. Shoot, he still has enough spunk in him to slap someone cross-sided. Ain't no harm meant."

"No harm at all," Billy added. "Folks in Clovedale Falls respect Barney, even if he does smell like mothballs. I'm sure folks have said I smell like cow poo a time or two but that don't mean they want to chase me out of town with a torch and pitchfork."

Rita didn't like the fact that Billy—at least it was appearing—wasn't taking her side in the matter. "Well, be that as it may," she said, throwing Rhonda a stern eye. "Uh, I believe it might be prudent if we skipped breakfast and went straight to the bakery."

"Oh, come now," Billy told Rita, "ain't no sense in skipping a good meal."

"That's right," Benita declared and began working on her

third banana. "Listen, girly, don't go being offended over me, okay? I have a talent for making lots of folks want to skin me alive. It's just my way, I guess. You just gotta cover my mouth."

Rita dared to look at Benita. "I'm...not offended." She spoke in a stern tone. "I'm...listen...you must know Billy and I are eventually going to get married, right?"

"Sure." Benita beamed. "Cousin Billy told me all about the old ball and chain deal."

Rita stared at Benita. "Ball and chain deal?"

Billy gulped. "What Benita means—"

"Marriage," Benita cut Billy off and offered Rita a friendly smile. "You're wondering how long I'm going to stick around and what my plans are?"

"Well...yes," Rita confessed. "Please do not think I'm being rude in wanting to know."

"Not at all," Benita promised and went to work on her fourth and last banana, leaving a trail of banana peels on the table. "Look, sis," she explained, "I'm down to my last dime and needed a place to crash. I had no one to turn to, so I called my cousin Billy." Benita threw a loving smile at Billy. "Billy has always stood by me...good man. Anyway, I figured I'd stick around and see if I can learn how to do some farming and...who knows, maybe find a place to live right here in Clovedale Falls."

"You mean move back home?" Billy exclaimed, nearly spilling his coffee as thunder erupted and shook the kitchen.

Benita polished off her banana. "Well, it's not like I'm going to become the next Judy Garland any time soon," she sighed. "Besides, Los Angeles ain't my gig. Too many weirdos out that way. I think it's time I settled down and learned a trade...like farming."

"But you're...," Billy stared at Benita's skin-and-bones face. "You ain't got no meat on your bones. Why, you couldn't lift a basket of apples."

"Maybe I can drive a tractor?" Benita suggested.

"A tractor?" Billy nearly passed out. "Listen, there's safety laws I gotta go by or the state will shut me down. No, ma'am, you stay away from my tractors. I remember how it was when Uncle Cayberry tried to teach you how to drive… plowed into a row of peach trees."

"Oh yeah, forgot about that," Benita said and shrugged her shoulders. "Guess I'm not much behind the wheel."

"Uh…honey, what are you good at?" Rhonda dared to ask and then said something that made Rita want to strangle her. "Maybe we can help you find a job?"

"Really?" Benita beamed. "Oh, hey, that would be amazing." Benita's thin face turned into a happy ray of light —very colorful ray of light, bless her heart, but a ray of light nonetheless.

"Sure," Rhonda confirmed and quickly caught a sour eye from Rita. "First we need to know what your skills are."

"Well, let's see," Benita said, grabbing her coffee and taking a few sips. "Too strong, Cousin Billy…go easier next time. I love coffee, but I don't want to walk around frizzing out all day."

"I made the coffee," Rita pointed out.

"Oh," Benita said and winced. "Well…what can I say? The foot is already in the mouth."

Rhonda grinned. Rita and Benita sure were going to become…interesting…friends. "What are your skills?" she asked.

"Well, I can cook."

"Nearly burned down your folks' home when you were fourteen," Billy pointed out. "Tried to make an apple pie, remember?"

"Oh…yeah." Benita wrinkled her nose. "Forgot about that. Poor Daddy. Never let me near the stove again."

Rita rolled her eyes. "Have you ever been a waitress?"

"Oh sure…bunches of times…never works out, though,"

Benita explained. "I can never seem to balance food plates the right way. People sure don't like having their food spilled all over their shirts. Kinda learned that the hard way."

Rhonda fought back a grin and began to speak but stopped when Rita's cell phone rang. Rita sighed, checked the caller, and looked at Rhonda. "It's Brad."

"Sheriff Bluestone," Billy explained to Benita.

"Oh," Benita said and worked on her coffee.

"I better take this call." Rita stood up, walked across the brown kitchen floor, and stopped at the back door. "Hello, Brad," she said.

Brad Bluestone was in no mood to be cordial. "Is this Rita or Rhonda? I can never tell."

"Rita. You called my cell phone, remember?"

"Oh, right. Is your sister around?" Brad asked, standing in front of his desk holding a cup of coffee.

"Yes," Rita confirmed, wondering what was going on.

"Good," Brad said, "because I'm going to have to call you back into the line of duty." Brad took a drink of coffee, looked around his small office, and shook his head. "A man was found dead last night, Rita. He was shot."

Rita walked her eyes over to Rhonda. "Who?" she asked in a voice that only Rhonda could understand. Rhonda slowly stood up and made her way over to Rita.

"A man who lived in California," Brad explained in his tough voice. "He was renting a hotel room—listen, I'll go into more details when I see you. Grab your sister and meet me at the station."

"We're at Billy's right now," Rita explained. "It would be nice if we could eat breakfast first."

"It would be nice to find out who killed this man," Brad fired at Rita. "Grab an apple and get to the station."

Rita was used to Brad's gruff attitude. He was a good cop —and a good man—and that's what mattered to her. "Of course, Brad," she sighed. "It's a stormy day anyway."

15

"See you in half an hour." Brad ended the call, looked around his office again, and then grew very silent. "Whoever killed you, Mr. Debkins," he said, "knew what they were doing. You weren't shot by an amateur."

Rita lowered her cell phone and locked eyes with Rhonda. "Brad needs to see us in his office."

"I understand." Rhonda nodded and then grabbed her white raincoat off the wooden coatrack standing next to the back door. "Billy, Benita, we're going to have to do breakfast some other time. Sheriff Bluestone needs to see us."

"What for?" Billy asked. He popped to his feet and moved across the kitchen floor in his work boots. "Everything okay?" he asked, looking at Rita.

Rita grabbed her pink raincoat and put it on. "I'll fill you in later," she promised, kissing Billy on his cheek. She then waved a careful hand at Benita. "Have a good breakfast."

"Oh, we sure will." Benita smiled.

Rhonda quickly scooped two purses off the kitchen counter. "We better go."

Rita looked into Billy's eyes. "Listen, honey," she said, "stay close to home until I find out what's going on, okay?"

Billy studied Rita's worried expression. "Sure...close to home, you bet," he promised.

Rita patted Billy's hand and then walked outside into the dark, stormy morning with her sister. "A man from California was shot and killed last night," Rita explained, hurrying through the heavy rain toward her SUV.

Rhonda glanced around, spotted the barn and a few work buildings, and then let her eyes fall down onto the muddy driveway she was walking on. "Benita's bus arrived last night."

"I know," Rita said in a worried voice. She looked over her shoulder, saw Billy standing in the back door, and offered a quick wave. Billy waved back and reluctantly closed the door. "We need to find out when the murder took place and then find out where Benita was between the time her bus arrived and the time she arrived at Billy's door."

"You don't think…I mean…Billy's cousin?" Rhonda asked, reaching Rita's SUV.

Rita walked to the driver's side door and then stopped, allowing the heavy rain to fall on the hood of her rain jacket. "Rhonda, we don't know who Benita Cayberry is. We don't know anything about the woman, who her friends are, if she has a criminal history. All we know is a man is dead right as Benita Cayberry arrives in town."

Rhonda turned and looked at the farmhouse. Could it be that Billy's strange and crazy cousin was a killer? "Well," she said over the sound of falling rain, "I guess we better go have a talk with Brad and find out what's going on." Rita agreed.

Inside the farmhouse, Benita watched Billy sit back down at the kitchen table, pick up his coffee, and then lock his eyes on the back door. Something was horribly wrong—and Benita had a bad feeling she knew what that something was.

chapter two

L loyd Debkins lay dead in a small morgue located in the basement of the county hospital. The morgue was, like all morgues, cold, creepy, and silent. Rita and Rhonda both hated the very sight of a morgue and despised the smell of disinfectant spray that permeated the cold air. And to add to the creepy atmosphere, the walls of the morgue were gray—cold, deep, lifeless gray.

"Well," Dr. Fleishman said as he pushed the stainless-steel bed holding Lloyd Debkins's body back into a dark hole, "there's not much to this man's death. He was shot by a nine-millimeter bullet that came from a Glock 19. The bullet, which is classified as an RIP round, is designed with little knife blades that expand and puncture the organs, and from the looks of Lloyd Debkins's heart, I would say the bullet did its job."

"I'm familiar with RIP bullets," Brad told Dr. Fleishman in his deep, tough voice.

"So are we," Rita said, anxious to find out any other details and leave the morgue.

Rhonda bit down on her lip as she folded her arms. "Whoever killed Mr. Debkins knows about guns and bullets."

She spoke in a worried voice. "Clean shot...deadly bullet... we're talking about a professional."

Rita watched Dr. Fleishman make his way over to a wooden desk sitting in the far corner. The poor man appeared exhausted. Of course, Rita reminded herself, at the age of sixty-three, exhaustion arrived more frequently than with a healthy twenty-year-old.

"Mr. Debkins was found dead at the Clovedale Falls Hotel in room 112, right?" Rita asked Brad.

"Right."

"No witnesses?" Rita continued, even though she knew the answers Brad was going to fire at her.

"None," Brad told Rita. "You've read my report."

"Yes, I have...but...." Rita paused as she struggled to find a spot in the morgue to focus on. "The Spring Festival starts in three days. The Clovedale Falls Hotel is full. Someone had to have seen something, even if they're not aware of what they saw."

"The Spring Festival is designed to attract people who are fifty years old and up...retired people...people on social security," Brad explained. "The festival is primarily a flower gig put on by the Clovedale Falls Flower Society."

"Regardless, Brad," Dr. Fleishman said picking up a brown folder, "the festival has gained in popularity over the years. Last year more than—"

"Four hundred people showed up. Yeah, I know," Brad informed Dr. Fleishman. He rubbed his thick gray mustache and looked at Rita and Rhonda. "I questioned all the guests staying at the hotel," he said. "I came up with zip. No one saw anything."

"Someone saw something," Rita insisted.

"We can't make people talk," Brad responded in a gruff voice. "That's why I called you two into active duty again. Lloyd Debkins was a retired government stooge. He worked for the IRS for thirty years, retired last year, and now he's dead. Why? That's what you ladies are going to find out."

Rhonda continued to bite on her lip. "Divorced…no children…retired at the age of sixty-seven…." Rhonda looked at Rita. "We need to check Mr. Debkins's hometown, search for friends, close relatives, find his ex-wife…talk to old coworkers."

"Hours of work." Rita nodded.

"Then I guess you better start burning up the phone lines," Brad huffed, "because you're on the taxpayers' payroll as of right now."

"Boy, that broken leg you got last year sure has turned you sour," Rhonda complained. "You haven't stopped being grumpy since."

"Tell me about it," Rita added. "Brad, you need to remember that Rhonda and I aren't obligated to work on this case. We are officially retired. Remember?"

Brad rubbed his gray mustache again. "And it might do you two some good to remember that I'm the sheriff. Now get to work!" he bellowed loud enough to shake the morgue.

Rita and Rhonda nearly jumped out of their skin. "Uh… yes, sir…we're on it…sir," Rhonda squawked. She threw a mock salute at Brad, grabbed Rita's hand, and dashed out of the morgue. "Man, is he ever grumpy."

"Something sure has been troubling the man," Rita agreed, "and I think it has to do with more than just a broken leg." She hurried down a long, depressing hallway that ended at a single employee elevator. "Let's go home and start making some calls."

Rhonda pressed a gray glowing button and waited. "I have a copy of the report in the SUV. While you make some calls, I'll jump online and do some digging. I'm sure we'll be able to come up with something by tonight."

Rita nodded and then grew silent for a few seconds. "Benita?"

Rhonda shook her head. "Glock 19…RIP bullet," she said in a troubled voice. "I just don't know. That woman doesn't seem like she can walk straight, let alone get off a clean and deadly shot."

"Tell me about it," Rita agreed.

"But?" Rhonda asked.

Rita waited for the old, creaky elevator to arrive in the basement. It was taking forever. "What if Benita isn't who she seems to be?"

Rhonda scrunched up one side of her face. "That's a stretch."

"I know," Rita agreed. "Billy can vouch that Benita grew up in Clovedale Falls…but after the age of sixteen, the woman's life is a blur to Billy except through letters and phone calls and an occasional visit. People can change."

Rhonda studied Rita's curious eyes. "Are you saying that Benita's story could be false and she might have intentionally wanted to make a visit to Clovedale Falls?"

"Perhaps."

"Maybe we need to have a little talk with Billy?" Rhonda offered. "Billy said he sent Benita bus fare money and food money. Let's find out exactly how."

"Exactly," Rita agreed. "Of course, I never asked Billy how he sent Benita money because it didn't matter at the time."

The old elevator finally arrived. The creaky, nearly rusted gray door slid open revealing a tiny room covered with old brown walls and a stained brown carpet that had never left the 1950s.

"Shall we?" Rhonda asked.

Rita gulped. "I suppose," she said and reluctantly stepped into the elevator. Rhonda followed on nervous legs. "Perfect horror prop," Rita noted with a grin.

"Don't say that," Rhonda begged and hurried to press the button with the letter "L" stitched on it. The creaky elevator door responded to the command and began to close, reminding Rhonda of a coffin lid closing in a scary movie.

Rita forced her mind to stop thinking about old horror movies and remain practical. After all, she was a cop—a retired cop, but a cop nonetheless. Sure, the case she and Rhonda had tackled in Vermont and Maine had been…a little unorthodox, but so what? They had come out alive and that's what mattered. Now it was time to settle down, put on her cop britches, and act like a trained homicide detective.

"We have to use every resource we have to try to connect Benita to the murder, Rhonda. If the woman comes up clear then…great. If not…." Rita looked into her sister's eyes. "Billy could be in danger."

"I assumed your mind was going to wander in that direction," Rhonda said, nodding. "At this point we can mark Benita as innocent. I just hope, for Billy's sake, that crazy woman is innocent. It would break that man's heart if his cousin turned out to be a killer."

Rita waited until the elevator reached its destination and then stepped out into a small, old-fashioned hospital lobby that reminded her of an old Southern mansion. The Clovedale Falls County Hospital wasn't a shabby place. A Christian organization owned the hospital and managed to keep it staffed with a team of three full-time doctors and several excellent, experienced nurses, and other staff members who knew their stuff. What was even more impressive was that the Christian organization kept the hospital in tip-top shape while managing to maintain an old-country-style atmosphere. Rita liked the hospital—and was even impressed by the healthcare the small but warm building offered. The only thing Rita didn't like was the basement…the morgue…and the old elevator. Even cops had their dislikes.

"Billy isn't a stupid man, Rhonda," she said, walking out into the lobby, "but I doubt he'll ever think his cousin is a killer."

Rhonda studied the lobby. She spotted three old men standing beside a newspaper stand sipping coffee, a nurse sitting at the front station, and a middle-aged man with thin hair climbing a ladder in order to change a light bulb that had seen its last day. All in all the lobby was clear and normal.

"I guess you can't blame Billy," she told Rita, aiming her feet toward a set of sliding glass doors, grateful to be wearing a pair of boots instead of high heels. Rita, who usually wore high heels in order to look nice for Billy, had decided to don a pair of sensible walking boots too. "It's still pouring...hoods on."

Rita flipped the hood of her rain jacket over her head and prepared to get soaked. "Umbrellas are such a nuisance but these rain jackets aren't exactly our friends," she complained, stepping through the sliding glass doors and walking out into a dark, stormy morning. "This rain is supposed to be going on for another week. The Clovedale Falls River is already showing minor flooding...mostly pastures. If Billy isn't careful, some of his fields might flood."

Rhonda followed Rita to the guest parking lot, walking quickly through the heavily falling rain. Rhonda loved the rain—adored the rain, actually. But when it was mixed with murder, well, a new taste entered the air that turned the rain into an enemy rather than a friend. The image of dark, wet alleys flooded with murder filled her mind...wet with a sinister rain that held a hungry mouth drooling with pain and misery.

"Hopefully we'll have this case solved before the rain ends," she sighed.

Rita glanced over at Rhonda and then stopped behind a gray truck. "In Vermont," she said out of nowhere, "we really went out of bounds, Rhonda. We broke every rule in the book in order to try and play the good guys—and we failed. I mean...what a disaster Vermont was for us."

"We came out alive," Rhonda reminded her sister, speaking over the rain.

"But we didn't do any good," Rita added in a miserable voice. "The killer who ended the life of my friend received a justice that wasn't legal." Rita shook her head, ignoring the rain. "Look, my point is, if Billy is in danger, I may not be willing to play by the rules. I know Vermont was a disaster, and I know I should have learned my lesson, but we're talking about—"

"The man you love," Rhonda cut in and offered a loving smile. "Sis, I know the game," she promised. "If Billy is in danger, I don't suspect we'll be playing by the rules at all." Rhonda reached out and patted Rita's rain-soaked jacket. "Look, sis, we both know Vermont was a mess, but we did try to do the right thing. I'm sure if we have to play outside of the rules again...we'll come out okay."

"Thank you, Rhonda." Rita smiled, feeling a tender sense of relief touch her heart. "You always know how to make a gal feel better." Rita reached out and hugged her sister. "As long as you're at my side, I'm always okay."

"Does this mean you'll drink from my Charlie Brown coffee mug?" Rhonda joked as she hugged Rita back.

"Not on your life," Rita laughed, patting Rhonda's shoulder and hurrying to her SUV.

A strange, funny little man watched Rita and Rhonda hurry to a white SUV, jump in, and drive away. He calmly brought a 1988 Oldsmobile to life and began following the SUV, keeping a safe distance.

Charlie "The Eye" Cook knew the crime business like the back of his hand. Having been in the private-eye business since 1978, the man had tangled with numerous dangerous foes including the mafia, and certain people in the mafia still wanted Charlie dead. Of course, Charlie wasn't a young, strapping twenty-year-old anymore who crawled through unlocked windows and explored dangerous, dark warehouses. Charlie was a sixty-five-year-old man who now earned his pennies by working for a private firm in California. But hey…a job was a job.

"*Amazing grace*," Charlie hummed to himself as he tailed Rita's SUV, chewing on a cheap cigar. Everyone who knew Charlie was aware that the man dreamed of living back in the 1950s forever. He even dressed as a private eye living out his life in a black-and-white movie. Charlie's favorite thing in the world was old hymns from the 1950s.

Ever the cop, Rita spotted Charlie's Oldsmobile tagging her SUV. "We're being followed," she informed Rhonda, turning onto Clovedale Lane Road and driving into a quiet, cozy neighborhood filled with warm gingerbread-style homes sitting in rainy front yards.

Rhonda checked the rearview mirror, spotted Charlie's Oldsmobile, and then calmly reached down and pulled out a Glock 17 that was resting in a holster attached to her right ankle. "Let's go for a little drive," she told Rita. "Start making a square grid and end back up at the hospital."

"Got it."

Rhonda quickly placed her gun down onto her lap. "I'll call Brad and set up a trap."

Rita checked the rearview mirror again and then eased off the gas until the SUV slowed down to 20 mph. Charlie backed off some, hit his right blinker, and turned into the driveway of a home that belonged to a family who was away on a cruise. Whoever was driving the Oldsmobile actually turned off the car and began to step out into the rain, throwing Rita off. By the time she reached a stop sign and hung a left, the driver of the vehicle was walking toward the house, wearing a dark gray fedora and a gray trench coat.

"Maybe we weren't being followed?" she told Rhonda.

Rhonda stopped dialing Brad's cell phone number, checked the rearview mirror, and then looked at Rita. "It sure seemed like we were being tailed."

"I know...strange," Rita said. "I'm going to swing around and check the car." Rita quickly made a square and moved her SUV back onto Clovedale Lane Street. When she reached the house Charlie had decided to use as a decoy, the Oldsmobile was missing. "We were being followed."

"By who?" Rhonda asked in a troubled voice as Rita slowly crept past the empty, rain-soaked driveway. "Sis, my gut is starting to really complain."

"Benita?"

"You bet," Rhonda confessed. "Why don't we skip going home for now and drive straight to Billy's. I want to get to know Benita Cayberry a little better."

Rita agreed. "We're on our way," she said, stepping on the gas.

Charlie, who was now parked two streets over at a stop sign, watched Rita leave Clovedale Lane and turn right onto Candy Stripe Road. He nodded his head. He wasn't a stupid man. "Benita Cayberry, it's time to pay up," he said, still chewing on his cigar, and took off after Rita once again, using extreme caution this time. Retired cops still knew how to spot a tag.

Billy was surprised to see Rita's SUV crawling down the bumpy, muddy driveway leading to his farmhouse. "Well, I wonder?" he said, standing inside his damp barn holding a pitchfork.

"What is it?" Benita asked, sitting in the shadows of the barn on a wooden stool trying to milk Old Betsy. Old Betsy, who didn't like anyone milking her except Billy, turned her head, gave Benita a sour look, and then made a "get away from me" motion with her back legs. "Hey, you ornery old cow," Benita complained, "all I want is some milk!"

Billy glanced over his shoulder into the barn. "Don't go to

fussing at Old Betsy or she'll never give up her milk," he warned and then focused back on Rita's SUV. "I wonder?" he said again and waited until Rita and Rhonda exited the SUV before raising his hand into the air. "In the barn, ladies!"

Rita spotted Billy standing in the doorway of his barn wearing a gray rain jacket over his blue overalls. From a distance the man looked…well…as backwoods as a man could be; the old baseball cap that was always perched on Billy's head didn't help matters any.

"How did I fall in love with a farmer?" Rita moaned as she hurried toward the barn. Rhonda followed, neither of them knowing that Charlie was parked out on the front road. "Thought we would come back and have some coffee," Rita called out to Billy.

Billy knew better. Something was the matter and he knew it. A farmer knew when a patch of corn was in trouble. "I was just feeding the milk cows some hay," he explained as Rita and Rhonda stepped into the damp barn. "Rain has put a hold on most of my chores. Reckon I can't complain much. Back's been a little sore lately ever since I slipped in the shower."

"You slipped in the shower?" Rita asked as the smell of damp hay filled her nose. "Billy, why didn't you tell me?"

"Aw, wasn't nothing. I just let my feet be clumsy is all," Billy assured Rita. "Wasn't the first time I slipped in the shower and probably won't be the last."

"I slip in the shower all the time," Benita called out from behind Old Betsy. "Hit my head so hard one time I forgot who I was for nearly four whole days. Mighty scary thing."

Rita searched for Benita, found the location the woman's voice had originated from, and then nodded at Rhonda. Rhonda nodded back and carefully began walking deeper into the barn. "Yeah, I bet that was scary," Rhonda called out, hoping to get Benita to talking.

Benita stuck her head out from Old Betsy, spotted a

shadowy figure walking toward her, and waved. "I'm over here behind this stubborn old cow. Cousin Billy is trying to teach me how to fill a milk pail."

Rhonda saw Benita waving at her. The woman sure didn't seem like a killer...but then again, a killer could be disguised as anyone, even a clumsy, crazy, kooky, backwoods gal with funny-colored hair. "I've tried my hand at milking a cow," she told Benita in a casual voice. "I didn't do so good. Now my sister, Rita...of all people...she can milk a cow."

"Hey, that's right," Billy exclaimed and smiled proudly at Rita. "I done forgot that Old Betsy lets you milk her."

"One time...one time," Rita claimed and held up one finger into the shadowy air. The last thing in the world a sophisticated woman wanted to be known as was...a cow milker. Rita was intelligent and enjoyed fine art and classic literature, and milking cows wasn't part of her...palette; however, Rita had to admit that she didn't do so bad milking Old Betsy. "Listen, Billy...how about a cup of coffee?" she asked. "Rhonda will keep Benita company while we go inside to the kitchen."

Rhonda stepped up to the wooden stall Old Betsy was resting in. "Sure, Benita and I will chat some," she called out to Billy.

"We could be chatting for years to come," Benita warned Rhonda, "because this ornery old cow ain't giving me no milk."

Billy looked into Rita's eyes and read something he sure didn't like. "Sure enough," he said with a nod. He tossed the pitchfork down onto a pile of hay and walked Rita out of the barn and toward the farmhouse. "Rain like this makes a man feel helpless," he told Rita in a worried voice. "My back fields are already starting to flood some. Went and checked on them soon after you left this morning."

"Did Benita go with you?" Rita asked.

Billy shook his head. "Ain't no room in the tractor for two," he explained, reaching the back door of the farmhouse.

Rita quickly opened the door, stepped into the warm house, and began shaking rain off her jacket. "How long were you gone?" she asked.

"Oh, about an hour or so," Billy explained as he stomped his work boots on the brown weather mat. "Benita stayed here and washed up our breakfast dishes. Can't say she did a good job either. Mighty worried about that gal." Billy paused, looked into Rita's beautiful eyes, and added, "Seems like I'm not the only one worried about a lame horse."

Rita studied Billy's eyes and then nodded. "That's true," she said, walking over to the kitchen table and sitting down. "Billy, the reason Brad wanted to see me was because a man had been shot and killed."

"I figured some sour weeds had appeared in town," Billy said and shook his head in disgust. "Shame that folks go around acting evil instead of good."

"Yes, it is a shame," Rita agreed.

Billy walked over to the kitchen counter and studied the coffeepot, which was half-full of old coffee. "I reckon I better make a fresh pot," he said in a troubled voice. "My gut is telling me this is going to be a long day." Billy turned and walked his eyes back to Rita. "I reckon if you decided to come back to the farm that means my cousin is in some trouble?"

Rita slowly folded her hands together. It was time to bring Billy onto the scene. "Billy, the man who was killed traveled to Clovedale Falls from California. He arrived yesterday."

"Benita left that there state." Billy folded his arms and shook his head. "Benita arrived last night."

"But she didn't immediately call you when the bus arrived in town."

"Yeah, I know," Billy said and made a strained face. "I reckon it would have been smart of me to just have driven into town and been waiting at the bus station, but I was busy working on my tractor in the barn. Replacing a clogged fuel line takes some doing."

"I wouldn't know," Rita confessed. "I don't even know how to drive a tractor."

"Ain't much to it. Just takes a little practice and know-how and—" Billy stopped talking when Rita gave him a *"seriously, Billy?"* look. "Yeah…getting back to Benita."

"I would appreciate that."

Billy leaned back against the kitchen counter. "You think Benita killed this fella from California?"

"I'm not sure," Rita said. "Billy, the man who was killed was shot in the heart with a nine-millimeter RIP bullet that belonged to a Glock 19. Clean shot…clean kill. If there is such a thing."

"Hey, I know about those RIP bullets…mean little suckers," Billy told Rita in a disturbed voice. "It's beyond me why they make those types of bullets. Goodness, if folks put as much effort into saving a life as creating ways to kill it, this world would sure be better off. I reckon that's kinda a moot point right now, though."

"Unfortunately, yes," Rita said.

Billy bit down on his lower lip. "Can't say I can see my cousin carrying one of those Glock 19s around. Can't say I see my cousin knowing the difference a nine-millimeter and a shotgun slug, either."

"I admit that Benita Cayberry does appear to be…kooky," Rita agreed. "But Billy, a man who arrived in town from California is dead. Benita Cayberry recently arrived from California. I'm afraid we have no other choice but to—"

"Arrest her?'

"No, no. Take her down to the station for questioning," Rita explained in a careful voice. "The man was killed at the Clovedale Falls Hotel. Brad questioned all the guests and the hotel clerk on duty. Unfortunately, he came up empty-handed. Right now, we don't have much to go on. Rhonda and I are going to do some digging on the dead man and see what we can find."

"You mean you're going to see if the dead man is connected to Benita."

"Yes," Rita answered in a direct and honest voice. "Billy, my main concern is that your life could be in danger. Right now, I have to assume Benita could be guilty of murder, which means I will do anything necessary to protect you. After all—" Rita drew in a deep breath. "—I do...love you, Billy."

"Aw, I love you too." Billy beamed. "You know this man's heart belongs to you." Billy unfolded his arms, walked over to the kitchen table, and touched the tip of Rita's nose. "I figured you were worrying silly over me."

"I don't want you hurt," Rita said, looking up into Billy's loving eyes. "You're my...my farmer."

Billy smiled and then sat down next to Rita. "And you're my girl," he promised, leaning over and gently kissing Rita on her soft cheek.

Rita smiled. "You're sweet," she told Billy and touched his face. "Billy, if Benita is guilty of murder I...you can't...stand in the way of justice, okay?" she pleaded. "You're going to have to let me do my job and help me every step of the way."

Billy leaned back in his chair and began rubbing his chin. "I just can't see that gal killing nothing more than a mean old wasp," he told Rita. "I've know her all my life—"

"But not really. Benita left Clovedale Falls when she was a teenager, remember?" Rita quickly pointed out. "A few letters, a couple of phone calls, and an occasional visit doesn't exactly constitute as keeping up with someone. She could have a whole life you know nothing about."

"Reckon that's true...but still," Billy said and made a pained face, "I knew Benita's folks...mighty good people. Hardworking...churchgoing...God-fearing people...the type of folks that raise their children the right way."

Rita leaned back in her chair and folded her arms. "Okay, Billy," she said, "let's assume for a minute that there is another possibility."

"I'm all for that," Billy said in an urgent tone.

"Let's say that Benita is in some type of trouble and that someone followed her from California. Let's say that Benita knew the murdered man and that the person she's running from killed him," Rita said. "Rhonda and I discussed this option on the drive over and decided it is worth considering."

Billy nodded. "That row of beans sure makes more sense than tagging my cousin as a killer," he said.

"Possibly," Rita said. "But Billy, we can't rule out that Benita might have been the person who pulled the trigger either. Either way, I fear your life is in danger. If Benita is the killer she might try and strike at you and if she isn't, then whoever killed Mr. Debkins might try and place a target on your back."

Billy continued to rub his chin. "A rock and a hard place, huh?"

"I'm afraid so."

"And you're thinking it might be smart if I packed a bag and stayed at your cabin, huh?" Billy asked.

"The couch does pull out into a bed."

Billy frowned. "I ain't the type of man who runs from trouble. I could no more leave my farm like a yellow-belly coward than I could turn into a pile of sugar just sitting here."

"I was afraid of that," Rita sighed, "which means I'll be sleeping on your couch, Billy Northfield, and Rhonda will be sleeping on the couch in the reading room."

"So be it." Billy nodded. "A man can't leave his home because of a little flood water."

Rita admired Billy's courage. "Okay, then," she said and patted Billy's hand, "it's settled. Rhonda and I will immediately move in for however long it takes."

Before Billy could reply Rhonda opened the back door and

stepped into the kitchen with Benita. "Stupid old cow," Benita fussed, wearing the kookiest-looking rain jacket Rita had ever seen. It looked like a box of crayons had melted on it. "I give up!"

Rhonda shrugged at Rita as she began shaking rain off her jacket. "Old Betsy kicked her."

"Kicked you?" Billy exclaimed. "Old Betsy might be fussy but she's not a violent gal."

"Tell that to my butt," Benita complained. "As soon as I stepped behind her, she kicked me square in the tush." Benita turned, bent over, and pointed a finger at her rear. "It hurt."

Rhonda slowly closed the back door, cutting off the rain. "Uh…coffee?" she asked in a disguised voice. In other words, she was asking Rita how to proceed.

"Maybe later," Rita said, looking at Benita with careful eyes as the woman returned back to a normal standing position. "Benita, I'm afraid Rhonda and I are going to have to take you into town to the sheriff's station."

Benita froze. "What on earth for?" she gasped even though deep down she had an idea.

"A man has been shot and killed," Rita continued. "And he was from California."

Benita nearly passed out. She staggered over to the kitchen counter and grabbed it. "Oh my goodness…."

"Is there anything you want to tell us?" Rhonda asked Benita in a cop voice that was neither harsh nor friendly. "Benita, now would be the time."

Billy studied Benita. "Listen, gal," he plowed into her, "our folks raised us with the Bible…the right way, so if you're in trouble or have done some wrong you better spill the beans, you hear me? I ain't in no mood for any secret keeping, you hear me?"

Benita stared at Billy with wide, shocked eyes. "Cousin Billy…I didn't kill nobody."

"But you're in trouble," Billy insisted.

Benita winced. "Yeah...I guess I am in trouble, Cousin Billy. I was kinda hoping time and distance might cure the problem. Guess I was wrong."

"Uh-huh." Billy nodded his head and then gave Benita a scolding look. "Done went and brought some poison ivy in on the bottom of your shoes, gal."

Benita winced again and then bowed her head in shame. Outside in the rain Charlie aimed a very high-tech listening device that resembled a bullhorn at Billy's farm, listening to every word being spoken. It was good to work for a company that had all types of fun toys.

Far away in the rain, a deadly killer lurked unseen in a rental cabin...waiting to strike again. "Benita Cayberry... soon," the killer promised. "Very soon."

chapter three

"Why didn't you call Billy right when you arrived in town?" Rita asked Benita, standing in a cramped office that smelled like pipe tobacco smoke and old coffee. The room, which had once been a supply room, had been transformed into a so-called Questioning Room, a windowless, stuffy little room that Rita found distasteful.

Benita rotated a cup of coffee back and forth across a small table (a card table of all things) with nervous hands. "I wanted to make sure...you know...I was in the clear, you know?" she struggled to explain. "I was worried someone might be waiting for me...and well...when I didn't see Billy... you know...I figured I'd take a walk and see if I was being watched. A gal can never be too careful."

Rita leaned back against the right wall and glanced at Rhonda. Rhonda was standing against the left wall with her arms folded, studying every word Benita was speaking with a cop mind. "And?" Rita continued.

"I walked around town, okay?" Benita confessed, refusing to raise her eyes. Rita and Rhonda were both smart dames. Benita wasn't ready to look into their eyes because she was afraid their eyes might be glowing with...doubt. Benita knew her story sounded lame and Rita and Rhonda surely weren't going to buy it. "I walked around town...boy...it was sure raining...but that was cool, you know? I needed time to think and kinda clear my mind, while making sure I wasn't being tagged."

"You didn't call Billy for quite a while," Rhonda pointed out.

Benita sighed. "I lost track of time," she explained. "It... was nice being back in the old town, seeing old sights that I grew up with. I guess I walked down memory lane more than I walked down Main Street." Benita finally decided to raise her eyes. "You know, it's not wrong for a gal to miss her home."

"No, it's not," Rita agreed, studying Benita's eyes. It was clear that Benita was assuming the worst—but Rita, as well as Rhonda, knew the nervous woman was speaking the truth. "Benita, who are you running from?"

"Oh no." Benita nearly bounced out of her seat. "No way! No, ma'am! I'm not going to reveal one single vowel...nope!"

Rhonda glanced at Rita and frowned. Rita bit down on her lower lip. "You're very frightened. Whoever is after you must be very dangerous," Rita told Benita in a calm, even voice, hoping to open a door that Benita might walk through. "It's okay to be scared."

"I'm not...scared of who is after me," Benita told Rita in a shaky voice. "I'm scared of eating a bullet." Benita drained the last of her coffee and wiped at her mouth. "Look, a weasel ain't nothing when it's not holding a gun, get it?"

"Benita," Rhonda stepped in, "allow us to help you. Please," she asked in a caring tone. "One man is dead...you could be next. Also," Rhonda added, "Billy's life is now possibly in danger."

"I know...I know...good grief, do I ever know." Benita looked about to cry. She grabbed the sides of her head as if she were preparing to rip her hair out. "Cousin Billy is a great guy, one of the best…and look what stupid ol' me went and did. But I promise with all of my heart that I thought I slipped out of Los Angeles in the clear…I was so sure I did."

Rhonda walked over to the card table and sat down. "Benita, who are you running from?"

"Nope, no way—"

"Yes way!" Rhonda snapped at Benita, startling the woman. "It's time to stop acting childish and put on your big girl pants, Benita. A man is dead and you or Billy could be next." Rhonda narrowed her beautiful eyes. "I hate to sound like this but you either talk or I'm placing you under arrest for murder, is that clear?"

"What? But I didn't kill—"

"Someone did and you know who," Rhonda snapped again. "That makes you an accessory to murder."

Rita folded her arms. Rhonda had taken the wheel and was charging through a brick wall. "You better talk," she warned Benita. "We will help you…but only if you're willing to help us."

Benita looked into Rhonda's stern eyes. "Rhonda…I can't talk…you have no idea. I mean, Los Angeles is a nightmare full of criminals. Don't you ever watch the movies for crying out loud? We're talking about crime, corruption…murder. I mean…the entire city is as criminal as all get out. The mayor of Los Angeles is a slime ball who won't do anything about it."

"My sister and I worked the streets of Atlanta for twenty years, Benita. We understand how big cities operate. The mayor of Atlanta wasn't exactly clean and clear either," Rhonda said.

"I've been to Atlanta, and Atlanta is nothing compared to Los Angeles. In Atlanta you have street punks, drug addicts, gangs, drunks, five-and-dime rats, small-time filth that keeps the Georgia prison system full. But in Los Angeles it's the big-time stuff—and I do mean big time." Benita grabbed her coffee cup and held it out to Rita. "More java, please," she begged.

Rita took the cup, left the room, and walked to a coffee station. "Well?" Brad asked, standing at the coffee station with Billy.

"Yeah, what's that gal spewing?" Billy demanded in an angry voice. "Why, I should take her behind the wood shed and skin her alive."

"Calm down," Rita pleaded as she poured coffee into Benita's cup. "She'll break. Give her another hour…two at the most."

Billy made a strained face. "It's a good thing her folks already went up to Heaven to be with Jesus," he said. "Why, if those good people were alive right now, they'd be so ashamed they wouldn't know what to do with themselves."

Brad patted Billy's shoulder. "Give the ladies time."

Rita looked into Billy's upset face. "I don't think Benita is guilty of anything, Billy," she explained in a soft voice.

Billy threw his hands up in the air. "How can you say that? A man is dead…and that varmint of a cousin of mine knew—"

"I think," Rita gently cut Billy off, "Benita may be a victim of circumstance."

"What?" Billy exclaimed. "Why, that sounds just plain silly…loony, even. All that gal is a victim of is being a downright liar." Billy began pacing around the room, back and forth past the four wooden desks, mumbling to himself.

Rita sighed. "He's all yours, Brad," she said and returned back to the questioning room. "Here's your coffee."

"Oh, thanks a heap," Benita said in a grateful voice, taking the cup of coffee as if it were gold. She glanced around. "Uh…any donuts out there? I'm kinda hungry."

"Later," Rita promised.

"Right now, we need to focus on the matter at hand," Rhonda told Benita, forcing the kooky woman to get her mind away from the thought of donuts. However, she had to admit some chocolate glazed or strawberry glazed donuts sure did sound good. "Benita, as of right now I'm leaning on the opinion that you didn't exactly mean to get yourself into trouble. Am I right or wrong?" she asked.

"Right all the way down the bowling alley," Benita assured Rhonda in a voice that could have exploded with anxiety. "I'm not stupid. Sure, my acting career was a flop, and sure, I didn't exactly become president—sixteen old-timers helped me run for president of their local drama club, but I lost by ten votes. Just goes to show that you can't trust people who live in nursing homes."

Rhonda quickly bit down on her lip. "Drama club? I thought you actually ran…uh…never mind," she said, resisting the urge to laugh. "Uh, Benita, what else did you do while you were living in Los Angeles?"

"You mean for work?"

"We can begin there, sure." Rhonda nodded as Rita leaned back against the wall.

"Well…I worked at the Green Mansion Nursing Home, a place for old and retired actors, writers, producers, folks like that," Benita explained as the sound of thunder suddenly appeared in the cramped room. "My, it sure is stormy."

"Focus…please," Rhonda urged Benita.

"Oh yeah…sure." Benita took down some coffee—burning her tongue in the process—and winced. "Ugh, way too strong."

"I'll put in a complaint with Brad," Rita sighed. "Now Benita, focus."

Benita put down her coffee. "Okay…I'm focusing," she assured Rita and Rhonda. "I got a gig at the nursing home," she began. "I was hired to read books, play games, take walks, those types of things, you know? I mean, old people need an ear to chew on too."

"You were hired as a companion." Rita nodded.

"Yeah…yeah, that's a good word for it. A companion of sorts," Benita exclaimed. "A gal I was rooming with worked at the nursing home as a nurse. She got me hired…sweet gal…but kind of…well…nuts." Benita made a crazy sign with her finger. "Thought she was the daughter of some foreign queen…real weird. But hey, she needed a roomie and I needed a roof and the price was just right."

"What was this woman's name?" Rhonda asked.

"June Bailey," Benita said before she could catch her mouth. "Oh…silly me. Now June is going to hate me for sure."

Rhonda rolled her eyes. "Benita, how long did you work at the nursing home?"

"Almost two whole years," Benita stated in a proud voice. "Boy, it sure was nice there. Well…it was until—" Benita quickly threw her right hand up and covered her mouth.

"Benita, please," Rhonda pleaded. "Talk to me."

Benita stared at Rhonda and then slowly lowered her hand. "We're not dealing with some five-and-dime punk," she said. "The person I'm running from is connected to some powerful people. Oh boy, we're talking about people who make the mafia look like schoolyard chumps."

Rhonda glanced over at Rita. "Government?" Rhonda asked.

"Worse," Benita stated in a hesitant voice. She grabbed her coffee, took some down, and then bit down on her lip. "Look…can't you just let me run off into the night like a scared raccoon and see what happens?"

Rhonda shook her head. "Benita, a man has been killed. We need answers," she demanded.

Rita stepped up to the card table. "Why don't you tell us if you knew Mr. Debkins," she said. "We can go from there."

Benita continued to bite on her lip. "I…well…maybe I did know him," she whispered in a tormented voice. "I mean… maybe the man was…sweet on me, you know?"

"Where did you meet Mr. Debkins?" Rhonda asked. "At the nursing home?"

"Where else?" Benita asked. "My entire life revolved around the nursing home. I had so many sweet friends there...except for that mean old Mr. Timer. He's the reason I didn't become club president."

"How was Mr. Debkins connected to the nursing home?" Rhonda asked.

"Oh, he was a privately hired CPA," Benita stated matter-of-factly. "Mr. Agatha hired Lloyd...I mean Mr. Debkins... about the same time I was hired. And as I said, the man was kinda sweet on me. But goodness, he was a dinosaur compared to me. I mean, seriously, what was that old coot thinking? I'm young and...vibrant...with lots of good years left. I couldn't tie myself down with a man who drank prune juice all the time."

"We understand," Rhonda said, nodding. "Uh...love is...difficult."

"Tell me about it." Benita nodded her head up and down, up and down, up and down. "Mrs. Owens warned me that marrying an older man would end up in disaster. Smart gal, that woman."

"Mrs. Owens?" Rhonda asked, soaking in every name Benita accidentally spilled on the table.

"Oh, Mrs. Owens was my gal." Benita beamed. "Used to whoop my tail at checkers...never won a single game." Benita took some more coffee down. "Mrs. Owens carried out a lot of supporting roles in those old cheesy B-movies from the 1950s that were shown at the drive-ins. She ended up becoming a screenwriter and writing some pretty popular cowboy movies."

"Sounds...interesting," Rhonda said. "Okay, so we know that Mr. Debkins was hired as a CPA, which makes me wonder if he was...an honest CPA?" Rhonda asked, deliberately throwing a careful punch at Benita to either dodge or strike at.

Rita watched Benita's eyes fill with shame. "Yeah...you gals sure are smart cops," she whispered in a miserable voice. "Nothing gets past you."

"Mr. Debkins was crooked, wasn't he?" Rhonda gently pressed.

Benita nodded. "He was stealing from Mr. Agatha... rigging the books...that kind of thing. I guess his retirement pay from the IRS wasn't good enough." Benita focused her eyes on the coffee. "I sure didn't know that rat was stealing from Mr. Agatha...and I sure didn't know Mr. Agatha—" Benita stopped talking.

"What?" Rhonda asked. "Benita, now isn't the time to clam up."

"How can I not?" Benita begged. She threw her eyes at Rhonda. "We're talking about the big time here, sister...major players...a ball park full of killers who have more money than Fort Knox. I'm...I'm a cooked goose."

"Not if you let us help you," Rhonda promised.

"Oh man. When I walked around in the rain and didn't see anyone I surely thought I was in the clear. Boy, was I ever wrong." Benita began banging her head against the card table.

"Benita...honey...stop it," Rhonda begged. "Benita... you're going to spill your coffee."

"I don't care," Benita moaned. "I'm dead."

Rita walked over to Benita, put her hand on the woman's shoulder, and made her stop banging her head against the card table. "Benita, the people you're running from own the movie studios, right?"

Benita shot her head up. "How in the world did you know?" she gasped in terror.

"Just a little hunch," Rita said.

Benita grabbed Rita's hand. "We're talking about people

who own the movies…the television networks…the news networks…the whole show. People who have billions…trillions…."

Rita patted Benita's hand and walked back to the right wall. Benita, she knew, was possibly overexaggerating the situation. If the movie studios wanted her dead the woman would have never left Los Angeles. No, Rita thought, sharing the same mindset with her sister, the person—or people— after Benita wasn't as big time as the woman was making out. But, Rita thought, a man was dead, which meant that Benita was being chased by someone who had been shaken out of an angry hornet's nest. "Benita, tell us more about the nursing home, starting with Mr. Agatha."

Benita gulped. "Mr. Agatha?" she whispered. "Do I really have to?" Rita nodded. Benita winced. "Okay…here goes."

"What now?" Billy asked as he gobbled down a donut. Powdered sugar covered his mouth and dripped down onto his overalls.

"Oh, honey," Rita sighed. She quickly grabbed a napkin from her purse that was sitting on Brad's desk and began wiping at Billy's mouth. Billy fussed a little but finally caved.

"I suggest we keep Benita here at the jail," Rhonda explained as she polished off a chocolate donut. "I'm sure happy a Krispy Kreme opened in Clovedale Falls."

"I'm sure happy I can buy a dozen of them there donuts and get a dozen free every Tuesday," Billy chimed in. "Chester sure loves his lemon donuts. That dog has put on nearly ten pounds since that there Krispy Kreme moved into town. Reckon I put on a pound or two myself."

Rhonda glanced down at her soft belly. The new donut shop had caused an uninvited pound or two to appear on her as well. "Brad, Rita and I are going to spend the night at

Billy's farm and discuss everything Benita told us. In the meantime—"

"I'll keep a constant watch on the woman and review the recording," Brad told Rhonda, reaching for a donut and nodding at a gray tape recorder sitting on his wooden desk. "The hour is getting late and that storm outside isn't letting up. Be extra careful driving out to Billy's farm. I already have three men fussing with downed trees."

Billy took another bite of his donut—and got white powder all over himself again. "No…honey…I—" Rita quickly took Billy's donut away, tossed it into the trash can sitting next to Brad's desk, and handed her husband-to-be a plain donut.

"But I don't really care for the plain ones," Billy whined.

"Eat it," Rita ordered through gritted teeth. Billy winced, smiled, and took a bite of the donut as Rita began cleaning his face again. "Like a big baby…," she mumbled under her breath as her hands worked to clean Billy's face.

Rhonda looked at Brad and grinned. Brad grinned back. Love was grand. "Well," she said and let out a yawn, "it's been a long day and spending four hours cramped up in that room with Benita sure didn't help my back."

"And it's going to be an even longer night, I'm afraid," Rita said as she finished wiping Billy's face. "We have to review every word Benita spoke to us, Rhonda."

"I know, I know," Rhonda said and went for a second donut—a strawberry glazed with sprinkles. "Maybe we can grab a pizza on the way to the farm?"

"How about soup and sandwiches?" Rita offered. "Something healthy…besides donuts." Rita took Rhonda's donut away and tossed it into the trash can. "One donut is enough. Those things are loaded with sugar and carbs… enough to drown an ant hill."

"Hey now, don't go insulting the Krispy Kreme," Billy objected. "A man and his donut do not part ways easily."

"Yeah," Rhonda jumped in. She grabbed another donut and backed away from Rita. "Krispy Kreme rocks my socks, sister."

Rita rolled her eyes. "Why me?" she moaned. "Why do I get stuck with donut addicts?"

"I'd rather be addicted to these here little donuts than to carrot sticks," Billy stated in a proud voice and then quickly polished off his donut. "Besides, I do enough work during the day to make an elephant need suspenders for his britches. A few donuts ain't never hurt me."

Rita pointed at Billy's stomach. "You haven't been working off your donuts in this weather."

"Well…yeah…but…when the sun comes out, I sure will," Billy promised and then shoved his hands down into the pockets of his overalls. "Yeah…reckon I better lay off the donuts," he admitted. "At least until the sun does come back out."

Brad grinned. Billy didn't know it, but Rita was training him how to be the perfect husband. "You guys better get out of here. I'll keep Benita under heavy guard and have one of my guys run down to the diner and get her some food." Billy began going for his wallet. "On the house, Billy."

"Oh…well…mighty nice of you," Billy told Brad and then looked down at his work boots with worried eyes. "Benita is nuts, that's for sure, but she's the tender type, you know? Don't be rough with her, okay?"

"You have my word that Benita will be treated with kid gloves," Brad promised.

Billy raised his head. "Mind if I go say good night to her?" Brad pointed toward his office door. "Thank ya." Billy grabbed a chocolate donut, left the office, and made his way down a short hallway that ended with a wooden door that opened up into a three-cell-holding area. Benita, stationed in the last cell, was sitting on a lumpy cot. "Brought you a donut."

"Ain't hungry," Benita pouted, curled up on the cot like an angry cat. "I thought I wasn't under arrest."

"Now, don't go be fussy," Billy begged. "Rita and Rhonda asked Brad to keep you here at the jail for your own good." Billy reached through the cell bars and presented the donut to Benita. "Brad is going to send one of his guys down to the diner to get you a meal. In the meantime, eat the donut, huh?'

"I ain't hungry."

Billy sighed, removed his hand, and looked at his cousin. "Now listen, gal, there's a killer running about, do you hear me? It ain't smart for you to be flying around free as a bird right now."

"But I didn't do anything…well, nothing too bad," Benita said, near tears. "Yeah, I know what Lloyd did and I should have reported him…but dog gone it, Billy, Mr. Agatha scares the pants off me."

Billy rubbed his tired eyes. "Yeah, I reckon a person doesn't think too straight when fear walks onto the stage. I was mighty upset with you…but I'm starting to understand your reasoning."

"Really?" Benita looked hopeful for the first time in hours. "You mean that? You're really on my side?"

"Half and half," Billy told Benita. "Rita and Rhonda are two smart gals. If you're lying, they'll find out, and boy howdy, you best not be lying, gal," he warned. "If you ain't lying…yeah, Old Billy is on your side. Family has to stick together."

"Oh, Billy, those are the nicest words anyone has ever spoken to me," Benita cried. "I knew you wouldn't kick me out into the rain." Benita jumped off the cot and ran over to the cell door. "And listen," she added, "when this mess is all cleared up, I'll learn how to become a real good farmer and earn my keep, honest I will."

Billy looked into his cousin's desperate, lonely face and

felt his heart break. "Eat your donut," he said and handed Benita the chocolate donut.

"I guess I better." Benita smiled, took the donut, and woofed it down. "I was feeling pretty hopeless earlier, but Rita and Rhonda...wow, are they smart. I guess they're trying to protect me. Reckon I shouldn't be pouting. Reckon I need to be grateful that they're going to help me, huh?"

Billy slowly folded his arms. "Can't say my heart is too anxious for those two ladies to face off with a killer," he told Benita. "Rita and me are due to get married come summer. If anything happens to that woman, I'll never forgive myself... or you," he added.

Benita dropped her eyes. "I'm real sorry, Cousin Billy...honest."

Billy sighed. "Benita, for the life of me I can't figure out why a beautiful woman like Rita wants to marry an old farmer like me. Rita is smart, beautiful, sophisticated. She listens to classical music and reads all them smart books. I read the comics." Billy shook his head. "I just ain't as smart as that woman is or as worldly, but for some strange reason that woman wants to marry me. Reckon I'm scared half to death as much as I'm confused and all...." Billy paused, rubbed the back of his neck, and then continued. "Rita and me have been down some dangerous paths. Nearly got killed a couple of times. Nevada...Maine...bad folks. I guess what I'm trying to tell you is that I don't want that woman...or her sister... walking in the shadows no more. And right now, there's nothing I can do to stop them because of you."

"I'm real sorry—"

"My point is, gal," Billy continued, "is that we don't have to care about you...but we do. Rita and Rhonda aren't helping you because they're being forced to...well, maybe at first, but not now. You see, they told me they've both kinda taken a liking to you."

"Really?" Benita's mouth dropped in shock.

Billy nodded. "I know those two gals pretty well by know and let me tell you, I kinda feel you're growing on them. So do your old cousin a favor, okay?"

"Anything."

"Swing the bat straight and don't go for any wild pitches," Billy pleaded. "And for the love of goodness, if you're holding anything back, spill the beans right now."

Benita threw her hand over her heart. "Cousin Billy, I told Rita and Rhonda everything. I spilled the whole pot of beans right out onto the floor, honest. Cross my heart."

"You better have, gal, because the woman this old farmer wants to marry is risking her life to help you," Billy warned. "And don't forget about Rhonda, either. Zach done went and proposed to her. Those two lovebirds have a future to hope for. Of course, we sure took a whooping in that there Cracker Barrel to ensure that future…boy, did we."

"Cracker Barrel?" Benita asked. "Sounds like a story."

"A very long story," Billy said with a sigh, remembering the black eye and split lip he had received in Alabama. "I reckon I better get. Brad will bring you some supper."

"Oh sure…supper." Benita nodded. "Uh…maybe a cheeseburger, no mayonnaise, with extra fries, slice of apple pie, some meat loaf, green beans, chicken and dumplings, biscuits, a salad, coffee, and a soda—"

"I best go give Brad my wallet," Billy said and then felt his heart break again when he looked into Benita's hungry, lonely face. "I'll make sure you get everything you ask for," he promised and then added in a gentle, loving voice: "I'm on your side, gal. I'll always be on your side. Old Billy wouldn't dare turn his back on you. From now on…well, you just consider my farm your new home."

"Really?" Benita asked as tears began streaming down her cheeks. "Cousin Billy…I don't know what to say."

Billy reached his hand through the bars and patted Benita's shoulder. "Just do what Brad tells you, okay?" he begged. "You ain't under arrest, gal, but you do need to stay put for your own safety until we can catch the fox in the hen house."

"I promise to behave," Benita told Billy, wiping at her tears and forcing a smile to her face. "Besides, what have I got to lose? I'm either going to be saved or killed. Might as well sit tight and see what the verdict is, huh?"

"You just keep your thoughts positive," Billy ordered Benita, patting her shoulder again. He said good night and then worked his way back to Brad's office. "Here," he said, yanking out his wallet and handing Brad seven twenty-dollar bills.

"Billy, I already told you—"

"Bring Benita everything on the menu, including some apple pie and a milkshake," Billy told Brad in a stern tone. "That gal is mighty hungry and I want her tummy full."

Brad stared into Billy's eyes and then nodded. "Everything on the menu," he assured Billy and held the bills up in the air. Apple pie and a milkshake."

"Mighty grateful," Billy replied. Then he looked at Rita. "We best get back to the farm. I have to check the backfields before I get off to bed."

Rita and Rhonda told Brad good night, followed Billy back into the front room, retrieved their rain jackets, and listened to the storm outside. "It's really coming down," Rhonda said, putting on her rain jacket.

"Sure is," Billy said. He grabbed his brown rain jacket, threw it on, and opened the front door. As he did, Charlie's Oldsmobile drove down the front street. "Now who is crazy enough to be out in this storm?" he fussed. "And driving an old Oldsmobile to boot."

Rita threw her eyes at Rhonda and then raced to the front door just in time to see Charlie's Oldsmobile fade off into the storm. "Rhonda, that was the same car that was tailing us earlier," she called out.

Rhonda ran to the front door and threw her head out into the dark, stormy night. "Any ideas?" she asked.

Rita slung on her rain jacket. "We find the person tailing us," she said in a quick voice. "Billy, you're with us. Leave your truck parked here. We'll come back for it later."

"You got it," Billy said, feeling a sense of excitement fill his chest.

"And here," Rita said, reaching her hand down into her purse and whipping out a Glock 17. She handed it to Billy. "Just take the gun off safety and fire."

"Wouldn't think twice," Billy assured Rita and smiled into her eyes. The woman loved him—and worried about him. "Ready?"

"Let's move," Rita said to Billy, nearly melting into the man's eyes. "Rhonda, you take the back seat. Billy and I will take the front seat. If any shooting starts, you shoot out of the back left window and Billy will take the front passenger window."

"You got it, sis," Rhonda said and hurried out into the rain with Rita and Billy. Three minutes later she was sitting in the back seat of Rita's SUV, soaking wet, but ready for action.

Rita jumped into the front seat, threw her purse into the back seat, barely missing Rhonda, buckled up, and brought the SUV to life. "Hold on," she yelled. She raced out onto the front street, hung a hard right, and began thundering down Maple Leaf Lane. "He couldn't have gotten far…could be circling," she said as the windshield wipers began fighting with the pouring rain.

"You know, I don't think the person driving the Oldsmobile is the killer," Rhonda called out from the back seat.

Billy, who still wasn't used to Rita's crazy driving, was holding on for dear life. "Why not?" he dared to ask, watching his life flash before his eyes.

"Why would the killer follow us?" Rhonda asked. "No,

whoever is in the Oldsmobile is following us because they think we have information."

"Private investigator?" Rita called back to Rhonda.

"Possible," Rhonda answered. "But until we find out. we should treat the driver as a threat."

Rita nodded, slid to a stop, and checked a four-way intersection. In the far distance she spotted a pair of taillights fading into the rain. "There," she yelled and peeled out, nearly making Billy wet himself.

Oh boy, Billy thought, it was going to be some night.

chapter four

Rita raced through the storm, flying over wet streets, screaming past sleepy homes, desperately trying to catch up to Charlie as the wheels on her SUV struggled to remain earthbound. Charlie spotted the SUV trying to catch up to him and began whistling a sweet Christian hymn as he threw his Oldsmobile onto a silent street lined with little gingerbread-style homes, kicked the gas, and sped off, managing to leave the street and turn onto Snowy Lane before Rita could catch up.

"Where did he go?" Rita said as she zoomed down the street Charlie had used as his escape route.

Billy threw his eyes out at the storm and began searching the sleepy gingerbread homes, desperately trying to get his heart to calm down. "Don't seem like no one has even sneezed on this street," he said.

Rita eased the SUV to a stop at a four-way intersection, looked to her left and then to her right, and sighed. "Snowy Lane looks just as silent," she said, frustrated. "This guy is good."

"And so are we...we'll catch him," Rhonda promised.

"Now just a minute...hold on," Billy fussed. "That there car we're chasing ain't new, right?"

"Looked like a 1988 Oldsmobile to me," Rita said as the heavy rain pounded the SUV.

"Good enough," Billy said, and without warning, he opened the passenger side door, stepped out into the rain, and began smelling the air.

"What on earth are you doing?" Rita yelled over the sound of the falling rain.

"Old car…exhaust…yep!" Billy yelled back and began walking away from the SUV smelling the air like a hound dog. "Just follow me!"

Rita turned and looked at Rhonda, confused. Rhonda shrugged her shoulders. "Who knows?" Rhonda said.

Rita threw her hands into the air and carefully began following Billy. Billy stopped for a few seconds and then looked to his right. "Ain't no exhaust smell that way!" he yelled, using the headlights on the SUV to highlight his hands as he pointed left. "Smell is going off in that direction!" Billy pointed to his right.

"You're marrying a hound dog." Rhonda grinned.

"Tell me about it…but he's a smart one," Rita confessed in a proud voice. "Billy, get in!"

Billy jogged back to the SUV and jumped in. "Sorry to be getting your seat all wet," he said as his hands grabbed the seat belt. "You best get a move on. That there Oldsmobile has some strong exhaust, but the smell won't stay in the air forever."

Rita nodded her head, kicked the gas, and took off. "We have to find this guy."

"Alive," Billy begged as his hands snapped on his seat belt. "Rita…this here rain ain't friendly to speeding vehicles. Best slow down a tad."

"No time," Rita said in a determined voice, leaning over the steering wheel and focusing on the road. "Billy, we're not far from the bakery. Snowy Lane dead-ends. You either have to take Clovedale Hill Road or Sugar Plum Street. Clovedale Hill Road takes you into town."

"Yep, sure does."

Rita nodded her head forward. "And the road is right up ahead," she said and began to slow down. "Jump out and use that nose of yours."

Billy tapped his nose. Yep, it was sure going to be a long night. "Just slow down nice and easy," he begged as his hands worked to take off the seat belt. Rita did as Billy asked, came to a safe stop, and waited for Billy to jump out into the rain. The poor man was most likely going to catch a very bad cold.

"Poor dear," Rita sighed, watching Billy hurry to Clovedale Hill Road and begin sniffing the air. "He's going to catch his death in this rain."

"Billy eats too much cayenne pepper to get sick," She promised her sister, using the headlights of the SUV to keep an eye on the man. "Cayenne pepper, turmeric, cinnamon… the man is a walking spice factory—and he's as healthy as a horse too."

"He didn't come this way," Billy called out. "Must have decided to take the other direction."

"Get in, Billy!" Rita called out.

Billy looked down a dark, rainy street that held more gingerbread-style homes, shook his head, and hustled back to the SUV and climbed in. "Okay, Sugar Plum Lane is down there to your right…nice and easy," he said.

"No time!" Rita kicked the gas and sped off before Billy could even close the passenger side door. The poor man nearly toppled out of the SUV. "Hold on!"

"I'm a holding…I'm a holding!" Billy yelled, struggling to pull his body back into the SUV. "Crazy woman, what are you trying to do? Make me road food for some vultures?"

Rhonda leaned forward and helped Billy get his seat belt

on. "Years of fighting through Atlanta traffic," she explained and then giggled. Poor Billy.

"Hold on!" Rita yelled as she slid the SUV onto Sugar Plum Street, nearly leaving the road and sliding into a tree in the process.

"Good grief, woman. Let us live for another minute or two!" Billy yelled as his hands grabbed the dashboard. "Don't kill us until I have time to make my peace!"

Rhonda, who was used to her sister's crazy driving, leaned back, folded her arms, and grinned. Poor Billy was getting a taste of what married life was going to be like. "See anything?" she asked.

Rita perched herself farther over the steering wheel. "Nothing...the rain is too heavy," she said, speeding down a road lined with two-story homes. "Sugar Plum Street goes for about a mile and then ends at County Road 33."

"Hey, that's right," Billy said, peeling his hands off the dashboard. "And guess what?"

"What?" Rita asked.

"Brad told me the Old Horse Bridge on County Road 33 is flooded. Plus, there's a couple of downed trees out there," Billy explained in a happy voice. "Looks like we've trapped ourselves a skunk, ladies."

Rita glanced over at Billy. Oh, she could have kissed the man. "Billy, you're the greatest," she said, beaming.

"Aw, ain't nothing." Billy blushed. "My nose and my ears did all the work."

Rhonda quickly checked her gun. "Rita, you better block off the road. Whoever is driving that Oldsmobile is sure to come back our way. It won't do us any good to spook him."

"What's your plan?" Rita asked as she eased off the gas.

"Block the road, turn the SUV dark, and then we'll hide behind some trees on the opposite side of the street, say, about ten yards up. When the Oldsmobile appears and cruises past our position we'll shoot the tires out," Rhonda explained.

"Say, that's a mighty good plan," Billy told Rhonda, sounding impressed. "You ladies sure are fearless, huh?"

"Just trying to be smart, Billy," Rhonda replied and then shook her head. "We weren't very smart in Vermont—"

"And I didn't exactly shine in Maine," Rita added.

"What in the world are you two talking about?" Billy asked. "Why, you both did some mighty fine sheriff work in both of them there states. Shoot, if I had my say-so, I'd declare you both shot forty out of forty." Billy reached out and touched Rita's shoulder with a loving hand. "I ain't never had a day go by that's been neat and clean. No, ma'am. Every day ends up with a few rips and stains on your clothes. Just the way life is, I suppose. So don't go kicking yourself because you didn't get a good load of wash done in Vermont and Maine. Just be grateful you lived to do the wash another day."

Rita looked into Billy's sweet eyes. "Rhonda and I played outside of the rulebook in Vermont because we wanted to help the town…and we made a mess of things. And in Maine…oh, what a mess that was."

"And in Nevada we ended the life of a snake bent on killing us all…so what?" Billy said. "Like I said, ain't a day that's going to go by that's going to end up neat and clean. Folks just do their best…and you two ladies always do your best." Billy smiled into Rita's eyes. "I was in Maine for the long haul, remember? I was in the storm. I saw how the story played out. You did your best…both of you did. Be proud… mighty proud."

Rita melted into Billy's warm, caring face. "Thanks, Billy," she whispered.

"Yeah, thanks," Rhonda added. "It's going to be great to have you as my brother-in-law. But in the meantime, we need to move." Rhonda threw the back passenger door open, stepped out into the rain, and studied the night. Rita quickly turned the SUV off, killed the headlights, and joined Rhonda. "You take the left side of the street. Go hide behind that tree up there," Rhonda said, pointing to a large pine tree sitting in the yard of a dark two-story home. "I'll be right across the street."

Rita nodded her head and waited for Billy. "Let's move, honey," she told him.

"Gun in in my jacket pocket," Billy assured Rita. He took her hand, and they hurried off.

"So sweet." Rhonda smiled, watching Rita and Billy run off into the rain. "They're perfect for one another."

While Rita, Billy, and Rhonda ran to their positions, Charlie stopped at a fallen tree that was lying over a two-lane back road known as County Road 33. "Not good," he said without becoming upset, and began the difficult task of turning around. Five minutes later he was driving back toward Sugar Plum Street. "I doubt they gave up the chase," he said and decided to pull over and park on the side of the road a few yards from Sugar Plum Street. "Might be wise to take a little stroll."

Charlie took the cigar he was chewing on, placed it in the glove compartment, checked his gun, and then climbed out of the Oldsmobile on easy legs that weren't in a rush to get anywhere. He checked the rain, studied his surroundings, and then began walking toward Sugar Plum Street humming "Amazing Grace." A few minutes later, after reaching Sugar Plum Street, he began moving through rain-soaked backyards, staying to the right side of the street—slipping through the rain unseen and unheard; the way of a true private eye.

When Rita's SUV came into view, parked across the street, sitting dark, Charlie nodded. "Not a bad idea," he said, impressed, standing behind a tree towering over the backyard of a lovely blue two-story home. "Now, let's find you."

Charlie eased away from the tree, circled back through two yards, eased around the side of a two-story brick home, and began searching the night with a pair of eyes that were more reliable than night-vision goggles. He immediately spotted Rhonda standing behind a tall pine tree with her gun at the ready. "Clever," he murmured. "Block me off…shoot out my tires…not a bad plan."

Rhonda, unaware that Charlie had discovered her position, studied the dark street with patient eyes. Sooner or a later, she assumed, the Oldsmobile had to return. Of course, waiting for the car wouldn't have been so bad if the rain had decided to stop falling. But, Rhonda thought, keeping her eyes focused, she did love the rain…and the snow…and spring…autumn and winter (summer, not so much). What was a little rain? Rain and police work always went hand in hand. A good cop loved the rain—adored the rain. Every mystery book in the world needed rain to flavor the pages; every mystery writer understood that rain was the vital spice needed to complete a grand recipe.

"Detective Rhonda Knight…standing out in the dark, rainy, night…waiting for the killer to appear. Is she scared? No. Is she frightened? No. Nerves of steel…heart of courage, Yes, those are the qualities of Detective Rhonda Knight," Rhonda spoke in an old-timey detective's voice. "Yes, when it comes to fighting crime Detective Rhonda Knight is always on the scene…criminals beware…"

"That might make for a good book."

"Huh?" Rhonda nearly jumped out of her skin. She spun around and found a short man wearing a dark gray fedora and a gray trench coat staring at her with his arms folded. "Hey…how did you…hands in the air!"

Rita heard Rhonda scream. "Move!" she yelled at Billy and tore across the street just in time to see a shadowy figure shake his head at Rhonda. "Hands in the air…now!" Rita yelled, aiming her gun at Charlie.

61

"I'm comfortable," Charlie told Rhonda and Rita in a calm voice. "Besides, this rain isn't too good for my joints."

Rita ran up to Rhonda. "Are you okay?"

"Yeah...uh...he just...appeared right behind me," Rhonda explained in a shaky voice.

"Could have killed you too," Charlie pointed out and then tossed his eyes at a large farmer who appeared beside Rita. "Oh, hello, Mr. Northfield. I'm glad you're here."

"You know me?" Billy asked in a confused voice, dripping with rain.

"Detectives Rita and Rhonda Knight probably know you better than I do, I'm afraid. But what I do know about you, well," Charlie said, smiling, "you're okay in my book."

Rita and Rhonda glanced at each other. "Who are you, sir?" Rita asked, deciding to lower her gun.

"My sister and I are assuming you are a private detective," Rhonda stated.

"Your assumption would be correct," Charlie replied. "I figured it was only a matter of time before we would be standing around the campfire together. I didn't want our meeting to be so soon, but a storm, a fallen tree, two determined cops...what can a guy do?"

"How about go back to my farm, dry off, and have some coffee?" Billy suggested. "I'm about as waterlogged as a duck that's been sitting in a lake for a year."

"Coffee does sound good." Charlie said. He smiled at Rita and Rhonda. "Perhaps we can swap dimes for quarters?"

Rhonda put her gun away. "Maybe," she replied. "It depends on what your intentions are...Mister...?"

"Cook. Charlie Cook."

Rhonda's jaw nearly dropped down to the ground. "The...the...Charlie Cook?" she stuttered in shock.

"You've heard of me?" Charlie asked with a slight grin.

"Who hasn't?" Rhonda tripped all over herself. "Rita, this is Charlie Cook—*the* Charlie Cook. Can you believe it?"

"I...no, I can't," Rita replied, standing in shock. "Mr. Cook...we've heard so much about you. I've personally followed many of your cases."

"Let's talk over coffee, my dears." Charlie smiled. "I'm not a young, strapping twenty-year-old anymore. This rain isn't good for a man my age." Charlie smiled at Rhonda. "Perhaps you would like to ride with me?"

"Really...gosh...of course." Rhonda beamed. "It would be an honor."

"Shall we?" Charlie put out his elbow. Rhonda happily took it. "We'll follow you," he told Rita. "Give us a few minutes to go get my car." And with those words Charlie walked off into the rain with Rhonda, leaving Rita standing in shock and Billy curious about his new friend. What Billy didn't know at that moment was that Charlie Cook was going to become one of their dearest friends in the world.

Charlie didn't take off his trench coat or the fedora covering his thin gray hair. No. Charlie Cook always wore his trench coat and hat, even in the presence of friends—and foes. Fortunately, Rita, Rhonda, and Billy appeared to be friends. "Nice kitchen," he said to Billy, sitting down at the kitchen table. "Reminds me of the farmhouse I grew up in as a kid."

"Where did you sprout up at?" Billy asked as Rita worked to make a fresh pot of coffee.

"Iowa," Charlie told Billy and then tipped Rhonda a wink. "Most people think I grew up in Los Angeles. I prefer it that way. Gives me an edge of...shall we say...mystery." Charlie smiled. "Besides, Iowa is boring. No one wants to write about a private investigator from North Falls, Iowa."

"So, you're a farm boy, huh?" Billy asked, spotting Chester strolling into the kitchen on lazy legs. "Well, look who woke up!" he declared. "Boy, you are one lazy dog." Chester flapped his right ear at Billy. "I don't care if you are mad at me because I forgot your donuts. You had a case of the lemon ones last night, remember? Doc said too many ain't good for you." Chester flapped his left ear at Billy. "Oh, it ain't my fault it's raining cats and…uh…it's not my fault it's raining." Billy shook his head. "Chester is mighty ornery tonight. Ain't happy that Benita was left in town. Dog has taken a liking to her."

"Benita Cayberry isn't a bad person," Charlie said in an easy voice and then held down his right hand. To Billy's surprise Chester walked over to Charlie's hand, sniffed it, and then wagged his tail. "Dogs have a way of knowing people better than humans do."

"Well, I'll be…I ain't ever seen Chester take up with a fella so quick," Billy said in a shocked voice as Chester licked Charlie's hand. "Looks like you done went and made yourself a new friend."

Charlie rubbed Chester's head. "Seems that way." He smiled as the smell of fresh coffee began to fill the kitchen air. "Can I bother you for a sandwich?" he asked. "I skipped out on dinner and my stomach is grumbling."

"Why sure," Billy said and shot to his feet. "I can cook you up some eggs and taters too. You just name it and I'll—"

"A turkey sandwich with a side of eggs would be good." Charlie smiled.

"Just tell Old Billy how you like your eggs."

"Burned," Charlie laughed.

"Burned it is," Billy laughed back. He hurried over to the wooden coatrack standing next to the back door and yanked down a brown apron that had belonged to his daddy. "How many eggs you wanting?"

"Oh, three should be fine. And maybe add a little cheese in with them?" Charlie asked. "And maybe a side of hash browns, some toast would be good too. And don't forget the turkey sandwich."

"You are hungry." Billy whistled.

Charlie blushed a little. He was hungry and poor. Being an old, worn-down private investigator meant less work. The company that had hired him to track down Benita Cayberry paid well—very well, as a matter of fact—when there was work to be had. Sometimes Charlie went months without work. Too bad he was paid per job instead of being tossed into a nice salary position. But that was the life of a private investigator—lonely, poor, and…yes…hungry. "Well, when I finish this job, I'll get a nice paycheck. Until then my pockets are filled with nothing but lint."

"Who are you working for?" Rita asked Charlie in a careful voice.

"I can't tell you that," Charlie told Rita and gave her a *"you should know better"* look. "What I can tell you is that the company I work for isn't interested in Benita Cayberry. The man who paid the company I work for to find Benita Cayberry is a different story."

"Dare I ask who this man is?" Rita asked Charlie as her mind began to reach out for the name *Ronald Agatha*.

"Not yet," Charlie told Rita in a professional but polite tone. "We have to switch dimes for dollars, remember? First, I want to know what information Benita Cayberry tossed out at the sheriff's station. I've been able to listen to your conversations here at the farmhouse from the road using a special listening device, but when I tried to lock on to the sheriff's station, I was unable to. Kept getting static…could be a number of reasons…I'm not really too technological savvy. Smartphones, internet, laptops, all that jazz is for the birds. Back in my day, a private investigator pounded the streets. Today it's all computers and fancy office buildings." Charlie pulled a cheap cigar wrapped in plastic out of the right pocket of his trench coat. "Back in my day, it was man against man…not man teaming up with computers."

Billy watched Charlie unwrap his cigar with sad eyes.

Charlie was an old-timer—a man who grew up in the old ways, the good ways. Sure, Clovedale Falls had gotten a Krispy Kreme, and that was sure dandy, but the town—for the most part—was still untouched by the outside world—a changing, cruel, hateful world filled with people who were possessed with a poisonous evil that was polluting mankind. The world outside of Clovedale Falls was fast-paced, filled with technology, smartphones, traffic jams, overcrowded cities, gangs, violence, drugs…murder. In Charlie's day, even though there had still been plenty of evil to battle, the world had been more…well, Billy thought as he walked over to an old-fashioned refrigerator and took out four eggs (Charlie was hungry and three might not fill the man's tummy), the world was more…simple. Neighbor knew neighbor, people said howdy to each other at the grocery store, the pastor came to visit and have supper, families still got together at Thanksgiving, kids still dressed sane instead of dressing like a bunch of mental fruitcakes that belonged in a mental asylum, little boys still played war and little girls still played with their dolls, the ice cream man dropped by every summer afternoon…yes, life was more simple back in Charlie's day; the good old days. Billy couldn't imagine the changes the man had experienced—and the sadness he now felt. "Time sure has changed."

"Yes, that's true," Charlie agreed as he placed his cigar into his mouth. "I remember when I was a youngster," he continued. "I wore out a pair of shoes a week working cases. I can't tell you how many miles I put on these old legs and all of my old cars. Back in my day a man had to use his brains and his back, and if he didn't, he was out of business."

"I bet you had some grand adventures," Rhonda sighed, lost in Charlie's eyes. "I once read that you tangled with the Alberto family."

"I was twenty-three, young and very stupid," Charlie informed Rhonda in a serious voice. "Donnie Alberto had my hands and legs tied together and threw me into the East River." Charlie shook his head at the memory. "That would have been lights out for me, but the idiot who tied my hands together didn't know how to tie a knot. I managed to get my hands free and swim to the surface just before my lungs caved in. Boy, that was a close one…sure taught me a lesson too."

"Oh, just like in the movies." Rhonda sighed again, propped her chin down onto her hands, and stared at Charlie. "You single-handedly took down Donnie Alberto."

Charlie studied Rhonda's star-struck eyes. "I broke into the man's house after he thought I was dead and stole a few files out of a safe. I turned the files over to the Feds, and that was that. No flashy fireworks, I'm afraid, no grand shootouts. No punches or car chases."

"Cop work is never flashy," Rita pointed out, aiming her statement at Rhonda. "Right, sis?" she asked in a stern tone, desperately trying to bring Rhonda back down to planet earth.

"Huh…oh yeah, right," Rhonda sighed. "Cop work is flashy."

"I said *not* flashy and…oh, forget it." Rita shook her head, walked over to the kitchen table, and sat down. "Coffee will take a minute," she told Charlie. "In the meantime, while Billy is cooking your meal, we can talk." Rita reached into her purse that was sitting on the table and took out five twenty-dollar bills. "Who hired the company you work for to track Benita Cayberry down?"

"Simple and direct. I like that," Charlie told Rita, taking the money from her soft hands and shoving it into his trench coat. "A man named Wayne Etterson wants Benita found before Ronald Agatha gets to her."

"Who is Wayne Etterson?" Rita asked.

Charlie chewed on his cigar for minute. The money Rita had spilled out would get him a nice hotel room and a hot shower, but he needed food money. But…Charlie thought as his eyes went to Billy, maybe his new friend might help out? "Look," he said and patted the money in his pocket, "I could strain you for money all night, but that wouldn't be right. The one hundred dollars you just gave me will put gas in my car and get me a room for the night." Charlie paused and waited for Billy to step onto the stage. And, as if someone had told Billy it was his cue, the man stopped breaking eggs into a green bowl and shot his eyes at Charlie.

"You needing a place to rest your head?" Billy asked.

"I won't lie," Charlie told Billy, "I've been sleeping in my car on the odd days of the week and taking a room on the even days. You see," Charlie explained as thunder filled the kitchen, "the company I work for pays me well…when there is work. When there isn't work…well, pennies get tight."

"But a man with your reputation?" Rhonda asked.

"I wish my reputation would make me rich." Charlie smiled at Rhonda. "Back in the old days my reputation got me all the work I needed. Today, the world is too fast, people don't even know who they are anymore. It's hard to keep up." Charlie switched his cigar to the other corner of his mouth. "A friend of mine got me hired on at the company I work for as a favor. I get assigned cases that involve older clients who came from my own time…mostly studio stuff."

"Is Mr. Etterson an older client?" Rita asked.

"Mr. Etterson is eighty-one years old, owns the Sunset Shine studio, and is heavily connected to a Katherine Finney," Charlie explained, deciding to give Rita and Rhonda a free slice of pie. Why not? They were nice enough gals.

Billy jumped in before Rita could ask any more questions. "Well, listen," he told Charlie in a friendly voice, "you can park your head here at the farmhouse. There's plenty of room. Zach is still in Alabama and Benita is resting her head at the jail. Besides, it'll be downright nice to have a friend under the roof."

"I was hoping you'd offer me into your home as a guest," Charlie said in a grateful voice. "When I finish this job, my pocket will be full of money and I can repay—"

"Not a penny," Billy told Charlie in a stern tone. "Old Billy Northfield wouldn't think of asking for a single penny from a new friend—not now or ever. My home is your home and that's the way of it."

"You better listen to Billy," Rhonda warned Charlie. "He can be very stubborn."

Charlie felt a warm hand touch his heart. It was rare to find a man like Billy in the world. "My wife would have liked you, Billy."

"You were...married?" Rita asked Charlie.

"Once," Charlie replied as sadness filled his heart. The image of a young, beautiful Japanese woman filled his heart. "I was married for twenty years...got married when I was twenty."

Rita saw Charlie's eyes fill with grief. "What happened?"

"Rita, maybe Charlie—" Rhonda began.

"No, it's all right," Charlie told Rhonda. "I'm growing into an old man and there's no harm in talking about memories." Charlie removed the cigar from his mouth. "My wife died in an airline crash," he said, moving forward in a careful voice. "We were flying to Alaska to visit a ski resort. The jet we were flying in...a 747 Boeing...one minute we're soaring through the clouds and the next minute we're taking a nosedive... seventy percent of the crew and passengers died...I lived. Why? Because when the jet took a nosedive, I just happened to be in the bathroom at the time. All I remember is feeling like the weight of the world was pushing me down...and then...lights out. I woke up in a hospital in Seattle." Charlie lowered his eyes. "Few bad cuts...a concussion...nothing serious.... Except my wife was gone."

"I'm so sorry," Rhonda told Charlie.

"So am I," Charlie told Rhonda. "But the Lord has His

reasons. It took me a while to understand that." Charlie raised his eyes. "My wife was a woman of faith and it wouldn't do me any good to doubt God's love, now would it? What happened...happened. All I can do is live and still try to do some good before the Lord calls me home to be with Him."

"Mighty fine words," Billy told Charlie. "Mighty fine words."

Rita looked deeply into Charlie's eyes. Charlie Cook—the world-famous private eye—was sitting right in front of her. Only, Charlie Cook was simply an old man carrying a sad heart and a few pennies in his pocket. Books had a way of romanticizing a man; life had a way of painting the true reality.

"Charlie," Rita said in a soft, caring tone, "it's getting late. We can talk more tomorrow. Right now, I think we all need to rest our minds."

"Wish we could," Charlie told Rita, "but we have work to do. Mr. Debkins is dead and the man who killed him isn't going to get his paycheck until he kills Benita Cayberry. If that happens, Mr. Etterson is going to...lose too. There's a lot at risk in this game and right now we can't afford to get lazy." Charlie grabbed his cigar. "My wife is in Heaven waiting for me, and someday I'll be with her. In the meantime, I have... we have work to do."

Rita and Rhonda looked at each other. "Okay," Rhonda said and focused her eyes back on Charlie. "Let's get to work."

Outside in the rain the man who killed Lloyd Debkins slowly drove past the sheriff's station. Yes. It was time to get to work.

chapter five

Brad wasn't expecting any action. All of his regular deputies were out on weather calls, leaving the sheriff's station nice and quiet. Benita was locked safely away in a secure cell with her belly stuffed and reading a couple of comic books. The station was blessedly silent, giving Brad the time he needed to review the coroner's report on Lloyd Debkins. Sure, he had reviewed the report numerous times, but there was something—something written in between the lines—that was bothering Brad, something he hadn't revealed to Rita or Rhonda.

"A RIP bullet...." Brad leaned back in his office chair holding the brown folder and allowing his mind to wander a bit. "Shot in the heart, but...the bullet entered the heart at a slight angle...." Brad closed his eyes, saw Lloyd Debkins standing in a room at the Clovedale Falls Hotel, and created a slow-moving scene. "Debkins is standing near the bed...killer pulls out a gun...Debkins turns to...run...and is shot...possible."

"Very possible," a dark voice told Brad.

Brad snatched his eyes open like a bullet. A tall, scary-looking man wearing a wet, black hood attached to a black rain jacket was standing in the doorway to his office. "Who are you?" Brad demanded. Whoever the man was, he had the advantage. Brad's hands were far away from his gun.

"Don't worry, all I want is the woman," Thorn Bedford told Brad in a creepy voice. "Now, why don't you take a little nap, Sheriff?"

Brad watched Thorn pull a strange gun out the right pocket of his rain jacket. A funny-looking dart was sticking out of the barrel of the gun. With no time to waste, he threw down the file in his hands and attempted to go for his gun that was resting on his right hip. Thorn simply aimed the gun he was pointing at Brad, pulled the trigger, and sent a red dart flying through the air. The dart struck Brad straight in his left shoulder. Brad winced in pain, grabbed at the dart, managed to rip it out of his shoulder…and then…as his hands went limp…the dart dropped to the floor…the world began to spin…grow fuzzy…and then…nothing but darkness.

"Very good." Thorn grinned, watching Brad collapse down onto his desk. "Very good indeed." Thorn approached Brad, handcuffed the man's wrists behind his back, and then located the master cell key that was sitting in the top right-hand drawer of the desk. "Very good, Sheriff."

Thorn left Brad's office, his rain jacket still dripping with rain, and—like a slithery snake—walked back to the cells on slow, eerie legs. He found Benita hard and fast asleep, cuddled up on her cot with a warm, brown blanket, facing the wall. The floor of the cell was littered with food boxes that would make a person think an entire army had come through there. The smell of cheeseburger, fries, meat loaf, coffee, and other delicious aromas lingered in the air, offering comfort instead of desperation. Thorn was about to destroy that comfort.

"Benita?" he whispered. "Benita…wake up…Benita…."

Benita didn't wake up. The woman was in a hard, deep

sleep, snoring up a storm. Yes sir, when Benita Cayberry was out—she was out; or was she?

Thorn stared at Benita and then quickly checked his watch. He had to hurry. One of Brad's dumb deputies could return to the station at any moment.

"Benita!" he snapped. "Benita…wake up!" Benita continued to snore. Thorn gritted his teeth. "Benita…wake up!" he hollered. Benita didn't budge. "Stupid…." Thorn put his tranquilizer gun back into the pocket of his rain jacket, unlocked the cell door, and stormed into the cell. "Benita, wake up!"

Benita slowly opened her eyes as her hands gripped the hot cup of coffee she was holding under the cover. When her ears heard someone unlocking the door leading into the cell area, she knew it was bad business. Brad wasn't exactly the talking type, all of his deputies were out on calls, and Benita had plenty of food to last all night. Rita and Rhonda had left with Billy. Whoever was unlocking the door was bad news—and Thorn Bedford was very bad news.

"Mom…no school today, Mom…not now…five more minutes." Benita pretended to moan, knowing that she had one chance to escape…or die.

"Wake up!" Brad growled, leaning down and grabbing Benita by her shoulder. As soon as he did, Benita burst into action. The woman let out a wild scream, threw her cover off of her body and over Thorn's head, shoved the killer backward, and jumped to her feet. Thorn stumbled backward, slipped on a food box, and crashed down onto the floor, swinging madly at the cover Benita had thrown over his face. As soon as he managed to get the cover free he was met by a cup of hot coffee that tore into his eyes. Thorn let out a shriek and grabbed his eyes, unsure if Benita knew he wore a specially made contacts; without the contacts he was nearly blind.

Benita didn't wait to find out. She burst out of the cell and took off like lightning, not realizing that if she had taken the time to think she could have snatched the cell key that Thorn had dropped on the floor, locked the killer in the cell, and been a hero. Instead, consumed with fear and panic, Benita ran to Brad's office, found the poor man lying unconscious—and assuming that Brad had been killed—went screaming out into the night and vanished into the dark, falling rain.

Thorn, who had no spare contacts on his body, struggled to his feet and—only being able to see blurry images before his eyes—used his hands to find his way back out into the rain and around the corner of the sheriff's building just as Deputy John Greenfield pulled up with a pack of donuts in his lap. Thorn struggled to a parked black SUV, crawled inside, and immediately reached for a black toilet bag that he had stuffed in the glove compartment. A spare pair of contacts were resting in the toilet bag. Thorn quickly changed out the contacts and then crept off into the night just as Deputy Greenfield walked into Brad's office and found his boss unconscious.

"You're dead," he promised Benita, driving away from Benita instead of toward her.

Benita, who had managed to reach the downtown area, dodged into a dark, wet alley and dived behind a wooden trash can that was, ironically, sitting at the back door that led into Rita and Rhonda's bakery.

"Oh my goodness...the sheriff is dead. Oh...it's Thorn...I should have known...," she said in a trembling voice as her teeth chewed her fingernails down. "Oh my...what to do...." Benita searched the dark alley, didn't spot anything but shadows and fear, and hunkered down even further as the rain tore through her funny-looking dress. "Why didn't I grab my rain jacket on the way out. Oh my...Thorn is going to kill me...." Frozen in fear, Benita decided to stay put and wait until daylight arrived before moving. But then she saw headlights appear out on the side street and, assuming the headlights belonged to whatever vehicle Thorn was driving, let out a horrid scream, bounced to her feet, and began slipping and sliding down the wet alley, flapping her hands in the air like a mad woman. "It's him…it's Thorn!"

Benita burst out of the alley and hung a hard right, running toward a sleepy neighborhood. Ten minutes later she located a cozy gingerbread house that appeared to be deserted (a house that belonged to Mr. and Mrs. Pappy, who were currently visiting their son who had taken a job in Missouri). Benita quickly ran around to the back door of the house and tried the doorknob.

"Locked…always locked," she complained as the dye in her multicolored hair ran down her face, making the poor woman appear like an insane circus clown that had escaped from a mental home. "Why do people lock their doors? Where is the trust?" she fussed under her breath. With no other option but to return back to the rain, Benita decided to check the small garage that sat next to the house. "Please be unlocked," she begged, running through the rain. "Please." Benita reached the front of the shadowy building and focused on the wooden door sitting next to the large garage doors. "Please…" she whispered and then began to try to open the door.

Before she could touch the doorknob, a low, growling sound made her freeze. Benita, like an iceberg slowly melting, carefully turned her head and looked down. A large, mean, angry dog—a stray mutt—was standing eight feet away, hunched down with its fangs dripping out into the rain. "Oh…nice doggy," Benita whispered, nearly wetting her pants. "Oh…very nice doggy…nice doggy. Aunt Benita wasn't doing anything wrong. You see—" The mutt let out a vicious bark, baring its teeth.

Benita let out a terrified cry and backed up to the garage door. "Please…be unlocked," she begged as her shaky hands reached behind her back and began fiddling with the doorknob. "Oh…unlocked…it's unlocked." The mutt took one slow, angry step toward Benita, preparing to lunge at her at any second. Benita knew she had only mere seconds to live. So she did what anyone would do: She let out a wild cry, threw the garage door open, and hauled butt inside, hoping to outrun the mutt. The mutt, seeing his prey attempting to escape, lunged forward, missing Benita by a nanosecond. "Oh my…that was close…so close," Benita said, begging her heart to remain in her chest. "Oh boy…crazy dog."

A dark, shadowy room that smelled of oil, sawdust, and time greeted Benita. Only a row of narrow windows attached to the garage doors offered any view to the outside world. Benita leaned back against the wooden door she had entered through, placed her hands over her heart, and tried to calm down as her eyes soaked in the dark room.

"I see that dog got after you too." A voice spoke through the darkness.

Benita let out a terrified scream. "Who are you?"

Fourteen-year-old Riley Hopkins, who was sitting in the far-right corner of the garage on a metal toolbox, tried to play it cool. "I'm Riley. Who are you?" he asked and then pulled a single cigarette out of the pocket of a worn leather jacket—unfortunately, the cigarette was broken in half. Riley Hopkins, as much as he desperately wanted to be, wasn't a cool 1950s rebel. No, he was simply a kid who was trying to run away from home. Sadly, he only made it across the street to his neighbor's yard before being chased into the garage by a stray mutt.

"I'm…uh…nobody," Benita announced, associating the voice speaking to her with a young kid. "Uh…what are you doing in here?"

"Stupid dog chased me in here," Riley told Benita, still trying to play it cool. "Been in this garage for two hours."

Benita slowly removed her hand away from her heart and

studied the dark garage. "Good thing the door was unlocked."

"Old Man Pappy never locks his garage," Riley informed Benita. "Shoot, he doesn't have nothing to steal except some old tools that aren't worth pawning. All the good stuff is inside the house." Riley studied the broken cigarette. "The house has a security system...loud enough to wake people clear across town if it goes off."

"Really?" Benita asked.

"Yep."

Benita placed her right hand on the doorknob and then removed it. She decided that whoever the kid lurking in the shadows was, he probably wasn't dangerous. Benita had a special way of reading people's voices...a way of knowing who was dangerous and who wasn't. Riley didn't sound dangerous to her. "Uh...got a cell phone?"

"Nope."

Benita drew in a deep breath of damp, oily air. "Well... looks like we're both trapped in here, huh?"

"I live across the street...I...." Riley put his cigarette away. "You don't live on this street. What are you doing around here?" he asked. "You wanting to break into somebody's house?"

"What? No...I was...," Benita struggled to answer Riley. "Listen, kid...I was taking a walk and that stupid dog got after me, okay?"

"Taking a walk in the rain...at this hour?" Riley asked and then laughed. "Lady, you must think I'm stupid."

Benita sighed, pressed her back against the door, and looked through the darkness. "Truth is, someone is after me," she explained in a voice that caught Riley's attention. "I was at the sheriff's station. Someone...managed to get to me. I barely escaped."

"Really?" Riley asked, feeling the hair on the back of his

neck stand up. "Someone got past Old Hard Knocks Bluestone?"

"Someone...killed...the sheriff," Benita confessed in a scared, creepy voice. "I saw him...." Benita cradled her arms together. "Look, kid, you better find a way to get home. I know the monster who is after me, and he's bad... bad...news."

Riley quickly stood up. "Uh...yeah...I live right across the street. But I can't outrun that mutt outside."

Benita studied the dark interior and then sighed. "Looks like we're both trapped, then," she told Riley.

Riley quickly reached into his jacket pocket and pulled out a small flashlight, turned it on, and threw the beam directly at Benita's face. All he saw before he fainted was a hideous woman covered with trails of hair dye that had mixed together, creating the face of an insane clown.

"A...monster!" he yelled and then hit the floor.

Benita watched Riley faint and then watched the flashlight roll away from his hand and land next to a pile of old boards. Then, assuming Riley had actually seen a real monster—unaware that the kid was talking about her—she fainted too. Of course, Benita couldn't faint with grace. The poor woman just hit the floor like a bag of wet sand, striking her head on hard, cold concrete.

Three hours later she woke in the emergency room with a warm white blanket covering her body. Billy was standing next to her hospital bed. As she would discover later, Riley woke up from his faint determined to get away from the "monster," mean dog or no mean dog. He found a deep freezer in the garage and found a package of steak. He threw the steak to the growling dog and ran home, calling the police and telling them about the "monster" in the Pappys' garage. And that's how Billy, Rita, and Rhonda found Benita.

Billy, who was standing with his arms folded and staring at a strange bunch of plastic tubes hanging from a wall, jerked, threw his eyes down, and spotted Benita opening her eyes. He hurried out of the room. "She's coming around," he called out to Rita. Rita was standing outside of another room talking to Rhonda. "You ladies best hurry...no telling how long she might stay awake for this time."

"You stay with Brad," Rita told her sister and took off running for Benita's room. Rhonda watched Rita vanish out of sight and then stepped into a room holding a very angry sheriff. Seeing Rhonda, Brad demanded he be given his clothes. Poor Rhonda simply escaped back into the hallway as Brad began yelling up a storm.

What a night.

"Why didn't you tell us about Thorn Bedford?" Brad growled at Benita as he rubbed his eyes. Whatever juice Thorn filled him full of was sure taking time to wear off.

Benita lifted her right hand and touched the white bandage wrapped around her head. "Are you sure I should have been discharged from the hospital?" she asked in a worried voice, ignoring Brad's temper. "I did take a bad fall... and my head does hurt."

Billy leaned back against the kitchen counter and shook his head. Sure, Benita was safely back in his farmhouse sitting at the kitchen table working down a cup of coffee, but that didn't mean he wasn't mighty angry. "You should have spilled the beans...all the beans, gal," he fussed.

"I know...I know," Benita whined and quickly took a sip of coffee. "But...Thorn...who knew?"

"What do you mean?" Rita asked, standing beside the back door watching a gray, stormy morning appear before her eyes as the last drips of a dark night slowly faded away.

Rhonda sat down across from Benita with a plain donut in her hand. Billy, the varmint, had scarfed down all the good donuts. "Benita," she said, "Brad could have been killed. Now isn't the time to withhold any more secrets, okay? We're all very exhausted and not in the mood to play ring-around-the-rosy."

Benita lifted her tired and worried eyes, looked into Rhonda's stern face, and winced. "I'm sorry. You know…a girl just…well, a girl has to keep some secrets."

Rhonda studied Benita's eyes. "I think I understand."

"Yeah…you're a smart one so you probably do," Benita sighed. "So go ahead and spill the beans…but with kid gloves. Leave me a little pride…please."

Rhonda took a bite of her donut and glanced over at Rita. "I think we have a sour romance."

"Sour?" Benita asked. "I'd say more like poison mixed with vinegar mixed with some TNT."

"We're all ears, Benita," Rita said, hungry for sleep. She left the back door, walked over to the kitchen counter, snatched up a blueberry muffin, and took a small bite. "Who is Thorn Bedford?"

Billy glared at Benita with a hard eye. "The truth, gal," he demanded, "or I'm going to put my work boot on your backside."

Brad, who was leaning in the kitchen doorway, rubbed his eyes again. "Get on with it," he barked. "I can barely see straight as it is…so just get on with it."

Benita made a pained face. Boy, was she ever in a mess. "Well…Mr. Agatha caught on to Lloyd's little charade," she began as her mind walked back in time and entered a stuffy little office sitting down a long, fancy hallway lined with treasures only the rich and famous could afford. She saw Lloyd Debkins sitting at an expensive mahogany desk that didn't go with the cramped office Mr. Agatha had assigned him. She saw a grumpy gray-haired man with cold eyes hunched over a bunch of financial files as his right hand danced with a calculator.

"Mrs. Owens told me, in secret, of course—Mrs. Owens and Mr. Agatha had once been sweet on each other, you see—that Mr. Agatha knew Lloyd was up to no good but couldn't prove it." Benita took a sip of her coffee without raising her eyes. "This is all secondhand gossip so I don't know how reliable—"

"Keep talking," Rhonda urged Benita as the rain outside began to fall harder and harder.

"Well," Benita said, "Lloyd wasn't stupid; I can give him that. Lloyd was what you would call…clever, you know? He knew how to watch his back. I guess working for the IRS all those years, you know, he learned a trick or two. Anyways, Mrs. Owen told me that Mr. Agatha hired a private investigator."

"Oh?" Rita asked as her mind walked back to Charlie. No one knew that Charlie was upstairs listening to every word Benita was speaking.

"Well, something like that." Benita shrugged. "All I know is that one day out of the blue, Thorn showed up at the nursing home. Oh…he was so handsome, so…debonaire. Black hair…leading-man face…real Jimmy Stewart type guy." Benita blushed, quickly took a sip of her coffee, and continued. "Thorn was hired on as a companion, like me, but he wasn't very good. Not a single resident liked him…not even Mr. Millstone, and that's saying something because Mr. Millstone liked everybody. Why, that man could strike up a friendship with an alligator and a buzzard at the same time and—"

"Honey, please…stay focused," Rhonda begged.

"Oh…yeah, sure." Benita blushed again. "Where was I?"

"Mr. Debonaire that nobody liked," Rhonda sighed.

"Oh…yeah," Benita said but kept her eyes low. Brad was sure steaming and she didn't have the courage to meet the man's eyes. Billy was mad too, but Billy wasn't so bad—Billy was family; Brad was not. "So, Thorn was hired as a companion…same as me, right? Sure. But none of the residents cared for him…oh well, it happens. The strange thing was, Mr. Agatha seemed to think very highly of Thorn, and that's when Mrs. Owens told me Mr. Agatha had hired Thorn to start watching Lloyd. Now I don't know if Mr. Agatha directly told Mrs. Owens; those two smiled at each other one day and fussed at each other the next…strange relationship." Benita finished off her coffee but didn't ask for more. "So, anyhoo, the next thing I know, Thorn starts to make sweet eyes at me—me, of all people. Boy, was I surprised too. I thought I was going insane. Why in the world would a handsome man like Thorn make sweet eyes at me?"

"Because Mr. Agatha thought you were in cahoots with Lloyd Debkins, that's why!" Brad barked. "It doesn't take a rocket scientist to figure that one out, genius."

"Boy, are you crabby," Benita fussed. She finally found the courage to raise her eyes and shot Brad a sour look. "I know I should have told you about Thorn, okay…I get that. But that doesn't give you the right to chew my neck off, pal, so take a hike!"

Billy tossed a thumb at the back door. "Brad, maybe you should go on home, huh?" he asked. "You're as ill as a rattlesnake and not helping smooth out the mud."

"I agree," Rita spoke up. "Go home, Brad."

"Don't tell me what—"

"Shut up and go home," Rhonda cut Brad off in a stern voice. "Dr. Ellison told you to go home and sleep this off." Rhonda looked at Billy and decided to take one of his famous sayings and throw it at Brad. "Now get out of here before we rub your face in the mud…and all that."

Billy walked to the back door and opened it. "Ben is outside in his cop car waiting for you. Best if you go get some sleep."

Brad knew Billy was offering sound advice. The truth was, all he wanted was sleep—but a killer was loose and he had a job to do. Still, Brad thought, barely able to keep his eyes open, it wasn't wise to carry out police work while feeling like a zonked-out idiot. "Yeah…I guess I better," he said and then looked at Benita. "Guess I've been jumping down your throat…sorry." Brad wobbled over to the back door, snatched on a brown rain jacket, nodded his head at everyone, and stumbled out into the rain.

"I best help him," Billy said in a quick voice and hurried out into the rain. He returned a few minutes later, soaking wet but content. "Ben is driving off with Brad," he announced.

Rita put down her muffin, grabbed a kitchen towel, and walked over to Billy. "Might do us all some good to get some sleep," she said as she began drying Billy's wet face. "I think we can wait until our minds are all refreshed and rested before we go any further."

Rhonda had to agree that sleep sounded nice. Besides, Benita was exhausted and pressing the woman about a sensitive subject while her head was wrapped in a bandage probably wasn't smart. "Listen," she told Benita, "you have to tell us all about Thorn Bedford when we wake up. Right now, it makes more sense to grab a few winks in order to get a fresh start down this path."

"Hey…sure…sleep," Benita said in a relieved voice. "My head is sure hurting…sure makes sense to sleep a little, huh? Besides, I might be able to remember better, right? You bet."

Rita stopped drying Billy's face and rubbed her eyes. As a young woman she had been able to handle long, sleepless nights. But now, as a woman in her early forties, her body and mind both cried out for sleep…and dealing with Benita Cayberry was going to require lots of energy; energy Rita just didn't have at the moment. "You're sleeping in the downstairs guest room," she told Benita.

Benita popped to her feet. "Home sweet home—"

"I'm taking the couch and Rhonda is making a pallet right

beside your bed," Rita continued. "If you try any funny stuff, it's back to the jail. Understand?"

"You bet!" Benita declared and grabbed Rhonda's hand. "Come on, roomie, let's get your bed made, huh?"

Rhonda sighed, polished off her donut, stood up, and walked out of the kitchen with Benita. A couple minutes later, Charlie appeared on the back staircase chewing on his cheap cigar. "Well?" Rita asked.

"Thorn Bedford works for the rich and famous," Charlie explained in a worried voice. "He used to work homicide before he went into business for himself. The man is bad news."

"I assumed as much," Rita told Charlie, fighting back a yawn, and continued as thunder began to growl in the distance. "I know we should have pressed Benita, but right now—"

"A tired man has a mind that is no good. I understand," Charlie promised Rita and then yawned. "We could all use a little sleep."

"Benita's eyes were having trouble staying focused," Rita told Charlie. "Brad was too ill to remain in the questioning session…." Rita fought back another yawn. Goodness, it had been a long night—and an even longer night for poor Benita. She looked at Billy. "Billy, I'm off to the couch."

"And I'm off to my own bed," Billy assured Rita. He kissed her cheek and wandered out of the kitchen on tired legs.

Rita pointed to the coffeepot sitting on the kitchen counter. "Cup of java before bed?"

"Sure," Charlie said. He left the staircase, locked the back door, and then sat down at the kitchen table. "Lloyd Debkins came to Clovedale Falls to retrieve a hidden treasure," he told Rita.

"I know," Rita replied as she worked to fix Charlie a cup of coffee. "In my mind, so far, it seems that Mr. Agatha might

have assumed Benita was working with Lloyd Debkins."
Rita took Charlie a green mug full of hot coffee. "When
Thorn Bedford showed up, Lloyd Debkins might have
panicked. All we know is that Benita left town...Lloyd
Debkins followed...and so did Thorn Bedford, which
means—"

"Mr. Agatha knew the escape route." Charlie nodded.

"Yes," Rita agreed, sitting down across from Charlie.
"Billy told me he used Western Union to send Benita bus fare
and food money. Looks to me like Benita was in a hurry to
leave town and didn't want to be tracked." Charlie leaned
back in his chair and listened as Rita caught him up to speed.
"The nursing home Benita works at requires all employees to
have direct deposit. Benita confessed that she was afraid to
drain her money because she didn't want anyone knowing
she was leaving town. She also confessed that her friends
didn't kick her out—"

"A smoke screen to fool Billy?"

"Yes." Rita nodded. "Benita Cayberry gets a two-week
paid vacation per year. Before leaving Los Angeles, she put in
for her vacation time."

"Smart."

"But not smart enough to fool Mr. Agatha, it appears...or
maybe it was?" Rita pondered.

"Are you implying that Thorn Bedford has his own
agenda?" Charlie asked.

"Charlie," Rita said in a respectful voice, "you never told
me who the man is that hired your company to track down
Benita Cayberry. Now is the time...please."

"I suppose it is," Charlie agreed as he chewed on his cigar.
"Ms. Knight, the man who hired my company to find Benita
Cayberry isn't Mr. Agatha. The man in question isn't really a
man at all."

"Oh?" Rita asked in a surprised voice.

Charlie sat very still for a moment and listened to the rain fall. When he spoke, his voice was very low. "Does the name Owens ring a bell?" he asked.

"Why, yes it does," Rita answered.

"Mrs. Lilly Owens…small-time film star turned writer," Charlie told Rita. He took a drink of coffee and then slowly folded his arms. "Mrs. Lilly Owens…grandmother of one Benita Cayberry."

"What?" Rita gasped.

"Does the name June Bailey ring a bell?"

Rita thought for a second. "Benita's roommate…the woman who helped her get hired at the nursing home, right?"

"A private investigator." Charlie smiled. "One of these 'modern' investigators who aren't very smart, I'm afraid. Ms. Bailey did well in securing Benita as her roommate and getting the woman hired on as a 'companion,' but nothing more. In the end she let Benita slip right through her fingers. Benita slipped through everyone's fingers, as a matter of fact, including Mr. Agatha's and Lloyd Debkins's."

Rita stared into Charlie's eyes. The man had tons of hidden information. "Charlie, all of a sudden I'm not very sleepy."

"I'm sleepy." Charlie smiled at Rita and patted her hand. "Chew on the bread crumbs I've just given you. We'll talk more after our minds are rested…and after Benita loosens her own tongue a little more. I need to ensure her story matches the knowledge in my mind. June Bailey may not have been smart, but Charlie Cook is no dummy."

Rita respected Charlie's professional attitude. It was nice working with a man who knew his stuff. "You know, Charlie," she said, standing up, "Rhonda and I handled a case in Vermont that we really messed up because we decided to play outside of the rules. I was worried this case might force me to do the same thing—because of Billy, you understand.

But now I can see that I'm going to be allowed to do my job as a cop…and that feels really good."

Charlie offered Rita a kind smile. "Ms. Knight," he warned, "don't get your hopes up."

Rita frowned. What did Charlie mean?

Only time would tell the truth. The simple case of Benita Cayberry was about to turn very confusing—and deadly.

chapter six

Mrs. Lilly Owens walked down a long hallway covered with an expensive burgundy carpet that smelled of time and memory. The carpet reminded Lilly of her own home—well, mansion—that still stood on Mansion Lane. The mansion that Lilly had once called home was now owned by a retired director who spent his days swimming and throwing ugly parties—a sick man who was desperately attempting to rediscover his youth by mingling with the younger generation and acting like an idiot, while turning a once lovely mansion into a crumbling garbage heap. Lilly didn't have time to worry about her old mansion, not yet, anyway. She was on a mission and Mr. Agatha was her target.

"Are you in there?" Lilly called out in an angry voice as she began striking a closed wooden door with a fancy cane with a silver tip. "Ron, are you in there?"

Ron Agatha let out a heavy sigh. Lilly was on the warpath and he didn't have any good news to calm to her down. "Yes, Lilly, I'm in my office. Come on in."

Lilly snatched open the door and stormed into the office, appearing old and angry—yet, still somehow retaining a lovely eloquence. Perhaps it was the pink and white evening dress or the way she allowed her long gray hair to run free. Ron wasn't sure. What the man was sure of was that Lilly still had his heart.

"You haven't come by to see me. Why?" she demanded.

Ron stood up behind an expensive mahogany desk that was surrounded by photos of Old Hollywood hanging on deep green walls that screamed 1950s. Some of the photos showed old movie studios, old movie sets, old cars, while others showed actual faces of known and unknown actors and actresses who had faded out of the limelight. "I'm afraid Thorn isn't returning my calls, Lilly."

Lilly glared at Ron with furious eyes. Oh, if only the situation were different, she thought—if only she had come to speak with a man who was dressed in a freshly pressed gray suit with his gray hair neatly combed and his old face still full of life. Instead, Lilly had come to bark at a man who was in deep financial trouble that was greatly infecting her own finances.

"I knew that man was sour," she snapped at Ron. She slammed the office door closed, wobbled over to a green-cushioned sitting chair resting beside a stone fireplace, and sat down. "What are you going to do, Ron?" she demanded.

Ron slowly sat back down, placed his hands together, and locked his eyes on Lilly. "Remember the old days, Lilly?" he asked. "Remember the studios…the sets…the sounds and smells…the people…the costumes?"

Lilly sighed. "Yes, Ron, I remember," she admitted in a sad voice that defeated her anger. "I remember the old days quite well. And before you ask…yes, I miss them. More than any human on the face of this planet will ever understand…I miss those days, Ron."

"Me too," Ron told Lilly. "That's why I was taking such a risk, Lilly…to get the money to buy us a studio." Ron unfolded is hands, opened a silver cigar case, and took out a very expensive cigar. "In my days, Lilly, I was a man who was respected, remember? When I said jump, people asked how high. I had powerful friends and money." Ron studied the cigar with sad eyes. "Now my friends have deserted me and the money is nearly gone. The money I make running this crummy home is pennies compared to the money I once held in my hands."

Lilly watched Ron put the cigar back into the cigar box. "Speaking of money, Ron, unless Thorn retrieves those bank codes, we will suffer. You will lose this…crummy home, as you so nicely stated…and those of us who love this…crummy home…will end up with no home at all."

Ron placed his hands together again. "I hired a man to get my books in order to please the IRS…and what happens? He discovers that I was laundering money through this home, stole my bank codes…." Ron felt his cheeks turn red. "I owe some very powerful people money, Lilly. I would blame you for bringing that girl here. She's involved."

"I refuse to believe that Benita had anything to do with this nightmare," Lilly snapped at Ron. "My sweet grandchild is as innocent as a morning rose. You're the one who hired Lloyd Debkins and it was that awful man who created this nightmare."

Ron narrowed his eyes. "Then why did Benita Cayberry run?" he demanded. "And why did Lloyd Debkins run at the same time? Explain that to me, Lilly. Explain to me that there are no such things as coincidences."

Lilly waved a dismissive hand at Ron. "My grandchild is innocent. I'm sure there is a practical explanation for her disappearance."

"I'm sure there is too," Ron told Lilly and then backed away from his anger. "Right now, I'm more concerned with Thorn Bedford and why the man isn't returning my calls."

"Yes, that is worrisome," Lilly agreed as her nose took in one nostalgic smell after another. Sitting in Ron's office was like being back in one of the old studio buildings she had worked in as a young woman. Oh, if only it were possible to go back through time—back to a time where the cars were young, the studios alive and blossoming, and people decent at heart. Of course, Ron Agatha had never been decent at heart and that was the divide that kept Lilly and Ron apart. Ron craved power and money—fame—even though the man, deep down, loved the studios for what they were, the same as Lilly. "If only it were possible to travel back through time," Lilly sighed.

"What?" Ron asked.

"I said if only it were possible to travel back through time, I would have never given my first child up for adoption. But oh…I was so young and so scared," Lilly said in a tormented voice. "The man I met in Georgia." Lilly bowed her head. "Howard was such a handsome young man…and I loved him so much. But…."

"But what?" Ron asked, curious as to why Lilly was confessing a painful secret at such a late stage in her life.

"Howard belonged in Georgia and I belonged in Los Angeles. Our marriage was very brief…less than a year," Lilly explained as a gentle tear rolled out of her eye. "I couldn't live on a farm and Howard couldn't live in a big city. When I left Georgia and returned to Los Angeles, I wasn't even aware that I was with child." Lilly wiped at her tear. "Ron, it took me all these years…and so much money…to locate my grandchild. I can't lose her now, but I'm too frightened to speak the truth. What if…Benita hates me?"

"Why would she?"

"Because I traveled back to Georgia and gave my own child up for adoption," Lilly told Ron. "I was hoping Howard would take my child, but he refused; he was so bitter toward me. I…was so scared, Ron…and so young…I didn't know what to do. So, I went back to the town I was born in—a little town called Clovedale Falls—and left my daughter on the steps of a church with a note…and ran away." Lilly dared to raise her eyes. "It took me many years to locate the good family that took in my sweet child…."

"This town in Georgia…this Clovedale Falls…seems to be a sour taste in my mouth, Lilly," Ron told Lilly in a displeased voice. "I would like to be rid of that town as soon as possible."

"Why?" Lilly asked Ron. "Clovedale Falls, as I remember the town, was always full of good, churchgoing, hardworking people. When Mother took me away when I was eight and moved to Los Angeles, my entire life changed overnight." Lilly placed her old hands together. "I returned back to Clovedale Falls one week after I turned eighteen…to attend my daddy's funeral. That's when I met Howard. Oh…I thought I could return home to the country. I so desperately wanted to go back to being that sweet, innocent eight-year-old little girl…but Los Angeles had already taken my hand."

"Yes, this town does have a way of growing on you," Ron admitted. "At least it did in the old days. The way Los Angeles is now…I must be insane to stay here."

"Why do you?"

"The memories," Ron confessed in a sad tone. "The memories, Lilly…nothing else. When I drive past the studios, down Mansion Lane, past the old diner, down the old streets, I remember…and remembering helps." Ron looked at Lilly. "That's why I did what I did, Lilly. For the memories. I thought if I could buy the studio…just one more time…one more movie…one more walk down memory lane."

"But crime?" Lilly asked. "Ron, you were laundering money for corrupt politicians."

"Yes, I know," Ron sighed. "My cut was twenty percent on every dollar. Lilly, I…think of the millions!"

"Think of your integrity," Lilly told Ron as her eyes grew sad. "Oh, Ron, can't you see that's what always kept us apart? All I ever wanted for you to do was live as an honest man, but even now, in our later years…." Lilly stopped talking.

Ron bowed his head in shame. "Yes, Lilly, I—" he began to confess but stopped when an old-fashioned black telephone sitting on his desk rang. "I better take this call."

"I understand."

Ron picked up the phone. "Hello?"

"It's me," Thorn said in a harsh voice, sitting in a dark hotel room in a larger town south of Clovedale Falls. "Debkins is dead."

"What?" Ron exclaimed, startling Lilly.

"He went for his gun. I had no choice but to kill the man," Thorn growled. "I went for the woman, but she managed to escape. I need more time...and money." The truth was, Thorn needed time to track down Benita, force the woman to give up the stolen bank codes, and then vanish into the wind. Of course, extra time meant extra money. Hotel rooms, gas, and food were not cheap and Thorn was not loaded with cash.

Ron took his left hand and touched his wrinkled chin. "Dead...are there any witnesses?"

"No," Thorn informed Ron. "I used a silencer. Now—"

"But Debkins might not have given the woman the bank codes," Ron cut Thorn off. "The woman might be innocent."

"Are you that stupid, old man?" Thorn growled. "Of course, the woman has the bank codes. Why else would Debkins have followed her to Georgia? Everyone knows he was sweet on the woman too."

Ron looked across the room toward Lilly. "Yes, I'm aware of that fact, but there is the possibility that the woman is innocent. Besides...I warned you...no killing."

Thorn threw his legs over a bed that was being soaked by cold air conditioning, stood up, and walked over to heavy brown curtains that were keeping the rainy day at bay. "Listen, old man, Debkins went for his gun, I didn't have a choice. Is that clear?"

Something in Thorn's tone concerned Ron. "What did

Lloyd tell you before you killed him?" he asked Thorn. "What did that man tell you?"

"Debkins—"

"No, you made him talk—and then you killed him. That's the way of it," Ron insisted in an angry tone. "Lloyd must have told you he gave the woman my bank codes…yes, that's it. That's why you went for the woman."

Thorn narrowed his deadly eyes. "Listen, old man, you sent me here to do a job, got it? What does it matter if I killed Debkins? I made him confess the truth and that's what matters." Thorn turned away from the window. "The woman has friends, old man. She has a cousin who has close ties with two retired cops. And to make matters more complicated, I saw Charlie Cook in town."

"Charlie Cook?" Ron nearly choked. "What is Charlie Cook—" Ron stopped and studied Lilly, who looked away from him toward the fireplace. "I think I may know the answer to that question."

"Charlie Cook is an old man…he's nothing," Thorn assured Ron. "My concern is the woman. In time I'll have her back in your office," he lied. "Right now, I need more cash."

"How much cash?" Ron demanded. "I'm not exactly loaded."

"A couple grand will do," Thorn snapped. "Hotel rooms… gas…food…running money. Get it?" Thorn rubbed his sore eyes. The hot coffee Benita had thrown in his face had caused damage. "Pay up or I walk, understand?"

Ron grew silent. Inviting Thorn Bedford to work for him had been a horrible error. Private investigators sure weren't what they used to be. Men like Charlie Cook…oh, those were the days. In the old days a man could pay a private investigator to do honest work and expect honest results. But those days were gone and Ron was now being forced to deal with rats like Thorn Bedford—a man who had come highly recommended but was a rat nonetheless. However, a rat—a bad rat—had a way of coming back and biting you. Ron knew that if he gave Thorn the boot the man might return to the nursing home and deliver a bullet with his name on it. "Two grand...not a penny more...and I want the woman alive. If she dies...you get nothing."

Thorn closed his eyes. All he had to do was locate Benita, force the woman to turn over the stolen bank codes, and vanish. Putting up with the likes of Ron Agatha was just part of the job. "Send the money, old man," he growled. "I'll call you in one hour and tell you the location." Thorn threw down the cell phone he was holding, sat down on the edge of the bed, and continued to rub his eyes. Even with a new pair of contacts in he was having problems seeing. "You're dead, Benita," he promised. "I'm going to enjoy ending your pathetic life."

Ron put down the phone and looked at Lilly. "You hired Charlie Cook to locate the woman?" he asked.

"I hired a company that employees Charlie Cook...and made a personal request, yes," Lilly told Ron, keeping her eyes focused on the fireplace. "I also gave instructions for Mr. Cook to stand clear of my grandchild and follow her—"

"To ensure her innocence?"

"Yes," Lilly confirmed. "If my grandchild is innocent—and I know she very well is—when Mr. Cook proves this, he will bring her back to my arms. But...if there is a slight chance that my grandchild is guilty...then I must know."

Ron leaned back in his chair, folded his arms, and stared at Lilly. "You're still a very shrewd woman, Lilly," he said, impressed. "Very shrewd indeed."

Lilly wasn't so certain. Deep down, she wasn't certain that Benita was innocent. Only Charlie Cook would be able to prove that.

Benita woke up after snoring a full eight hours through, nearly driving poor Rhonda insane. Rhonda, after trying to pull a pillow through her ears, finally gave up the fight, grabbed her cover, and went out into the living room and crashed on the floor. "My aching back," Rhonda moaned as she stumbled into the kitchen. "Oh, what time is it?"

"A little after 3:00 p.m.," Rita told her broken sister. "Here."

"My jacket? Where are we going?" Rhonda asked.

"Home," Charlie said, sitting at the kitchen table working on a cup of coffee. "Billy and I will watch Benita."

"Billy is in the barn milking Old Betsy. He'll be along shortly," Rita explained and then touched her hair. "Rhonda, my hair is a mess. I'm wearing the same clothes from yesterday. I'm a mess. I want a hot shower and a few hours of decent sleep." Rita rubbed her back. "That couch...lumpy."

"Try the floor," Rhonda complained, taking her jacket from Rhonda. She then grabbed her purse. "Charlie, are you sure?"

Charlie reached into the pocket of his trench coat and pulled out a deadly gun. "I'm sure," he assured Rhonda. "Besides, I set up motion detector sensors all around the outside of the house. The farm is too big to monitor, but I can monitor the house with clear eyes."

"Benita will be fine," Rita promised Rhonda as she opened the back door and studied a hard falling rain. "This rain is never going to stop. Billy said the back fields are now a lake. He's worried."

Rhonda looked out into a dark, gray day and studied the hard falling rain. "I bet our own backyard might be flooded too," she sighed. "The river floods when it rains a lot."

"Another reason I want to go home," Rita said in an urgent voice. "Let's move. Charlie, we'll be back around midnight."

"I'm sure we'll be here," Charlie told Rita. "In the

meantime, please don't be upset if I question Benita Cayberry."

"Not at all," Rita answered Charlie, putting the hood of her jacket over her head. "We would stay and question Benita, but we have our home to worry about. If the river behind our house is flooding…."

"I understand," Charlie said in a supportive tone. "Maybe by the time you return, Benita will have revealed some very useful information."

Rhonda studied Charlie's face. As she did, a strange sensation washed over her tired body. "Charlie…you're searching for something, aren't you?" she asked.

"The truth," Charlie told Rhonda in a voice that only an experienced, seasoned private detective could speak with. "While it may be true that Benita Cayberry did talk to you last night, we have to understand that the words that woman spoke may not be the words we need to hear."

Rhonda couldn't stop staring into Charlie's eyes. "What truth are you after, Charlie?"

Charlie lifted his left hand and touched his heart. "This truth…for the sake of an old woman."

"I'll explain on the way home," Rita promised. She grabbed her sister's hand, and they both ran out into the rain. "I know we're in the middle of a homicide investigation, but right now our home could be flooded," she told Rhonda, speaking over the falling rain. "We might have a very serious problem waiting for us at home. If the river isn't flooding, then we can rest for a few hours and get our minds back on track."

Rhonda tossed an eye back at the farmhouse as Rita dragged her through the rain and then focused her attention on the barn. Somewhere within the deep bowels of the barn Billy was milking an old, stubborn cow—a simple chore in a very complicated world. "Bye, Billy!" she yelled, hoping her voice reached the ears of her future brother-in-law.

"Be careful, now!" Billy's voice stormed out of the barn just loud enough for Rita and Rhonda to hear.

Rita jumped into her SUV, buckled up, waited for Rhonda, and then began a long and anxious drive back home. "The weather report said this storm front isn't going anywhere," she explained to Rhonda as she crawled down the long, muddy driveway. "I'm very worried the river might be flooding."

"We'll know soon enough," Rhonda told Rita, then leaned back in her seat and sighed. "I'm more worried about my poor back."

"Tell me about it," Rita complained. "I love Billy, but honestly, the furniture in his house is…horrendous."

"Old farmhouse…old furniture," Rhonda replied.

"Well, when Billy and I get married, I'm going to at least bring my bed," Rita stated in a determined voice and waited until the SUV reached the soaking wet back road before continuing. "Lilly Owens hired Charlie Cook to find Benita, sis. But I have a feeling you know that?"

Rhonda nodded. "The way Benita talked about Mrs. Owens…something in her eyes. At first, I thought Ron Agatha hired Charlie, but last night, as I lay awake listening to Benita snore up a storm, I kept thinking about what she told us about Mrs. Owens."

"About how Mrs. Owens gave her money…pampered her…bought her gifts…."

"Exactly," Rhonda said, nodding. "But what cinched it for me was how Mrs. Owens confided in Benita—almost as if she were warning Benita to be careful. I mean, Mrs. Owens confessed that Ron Agatha hired a private investigator. How did she even know that? And why would she even tell Benita? No…this Mrs. Owens woman stood out like a sore thumb."

"To you," Rita said, sounding disappointed with herself.

"When Charlie confessed who had hired him earlier this morning, I was shocked."

"Why?" Rhonda asked. "Sis, your mind is focused on Ron Agatha. My mind is roaming around with all the side characters. That's the way we work sometimes." Rhonda rubbed the back of her neck. "And speaking of Ron Agatha, what have you come up with?"

"Crime," Rita told Rhonda as she leaned forward on the steering wheel in order to see the road better. "Lloyd Debkins wasn't stealing money from a nursing home, Rhonda—at least not in the way Benita believes. Why would a retired IRS crumb bag risk his pension stealing pennies from a nursing home for the rich and famous? We're not talking about a payload here." Rita struggled to see the road through the heavily falling rain. "It's my theory that Ron Agatha was conducting some form of criminal activity and Lloyd Debkins somehow came across the cash flow."

"Makes sense." Rita nodded.

Rita eased off the gas as the SUV hit a deep puddle of water sitting in the road. "Ron Agatha hired Thorn Bedford to find out what Lloyd knew," she continued after speeding up again. "Ron Agatha could have simply had Lloyd Debkins killed."

"That's a no-no," Rhonda stated. "In the world of crime, it's a bad no-no to kill your enemy before finding out what goods they have on you."

"Exactly," Rita agreed. "Ron Agatha needed to know what Lloyd Debkins was doing in the shadows. My theory is Lloyd Debkins was stealing money—but in a clever way—from Ron Agatha's criminal fund. When Thorn Bedford hit the scene, the man panicked."

"And placed the blame on Benita?"

"Possibly." Rita nodded. "Something happened to scare Benita enough to make the woman run. The question is, what?" Rita focused on the road for a minute. "I believe it's possible Lloyd Debkins blackmailed Benita, sis."

"Yeah, all the words Benita was flowing into the air last night didn't seem very useful. Little tidbits of gold in the dust, but nothing to jump through a ring of fire over."

"What's interesting is that Thorn Bedford didn't kill Brad—and thank the Lord for that mercy," Rita stated. "Thorn Bedford could have killed Brad...why didn't he? Why did he kill Lloyd Debkins?"

"What are you implying?" Rhonda asked.

"Maybe Thorn Bedford didn't intentionally kill Lloyd Debkins. Maybe Lloyd forced Thorn to shoot him. I honestly can't say at this moment if I have confidence in that theory, though. All I do know is that it clearly appears that Thorn Bedford wanted Benita alive—"

"Which means he believes the woman has vital information," Rhonda finished.

Rita nodded. "Lloyd Debkins is dead. Why did Thorn Bedford go after Benita unless he believed the woman had the hidden treasure?"

Rhonda glanced over at her sister. "Do you believe Benita is lying to us?"

"No," Rita stated in a firm voice. "But I do believe she is holding back."

Rhonda leaned her head back. "You know, sis," she said in a tired voice, "we're supposed to be retired, but so far we haven't been able to enjoy our retirement. We've been caught up in one murder case after another. And now look at us, right back in the middle of the cake mix. I thought Clovedale Falls was supposed to be a pleasant community where the sidewalks roll up when the sun sets."

"And just think," Rita added, "all of this is taking place while you and I are finally, after all these years, planning our very own weddings."

"Weddings...." Rhonda let out a heavy sigh. "Rita, when

Zach proposed to me, I nearly fainted. I couldn't believe it. I thought I was dreaming." Rhonda turned her head and looked at Rita's sleepy face. "And money…Zach is inheriting more money than I thought I would ever see. It's all like a dream. Retiring, all these murder cases, love, marriage…it seems like just yesterday that you and I were sitting outside a warehouse in Atlanta on stakeout…and the next thing, we're trying to solve a murder up at Clovedale Falls Retirement Home. And how strange was that case?"

"A lot of twists and turns," Rita agreed. "Sometimes I wonder if we handled that case properly."

"We were thrust into a deadly situation and did the best we could."

"True," Rita agreed as she worked the SUV through another deep puddle in the road. "Throughout our career we always had people to answer to. And now we're free as birds to work on any case we see fit. The only person we have to answer to is Brad, and he's not too bad. It feels…alien…that we can work on a homicide case without all the yellow tape and bureaucrats breathing down our neck."

"When we first became cops, it wasn't so bad."

"Atlanta was bad," Rita pointed out. "Atlanta has always been a bad place."

"A lot worse today than it was yesterday."

"I know," Rita said, nodding. "I—" Rita suddenly stopped speaking when she saw a black SUV suddenly appear in the rearview mirror. The SUV was approaching fast. "We have company!" Rita called out.

Rhonda checked the rearview mirror, spotted the black SUV, and went for her gun as Rita stomped on the gas pedal.

When Thorn spotted the SUV, he was chasing gain speed. He hit the gas and managed to ram the back fender. The force of the impact caused Rita's SUV to start fishtailing.

"Hold the wheel!" Rhonda screamed as she rolled down the passenger side window and began firing at the black SUV.

Three bullets struck the windshield, causing Thorn to back off. Unfortunately, Rita couldn't get control of the SUV. Before Rhonda could pull her head back through the window, the SUV lost full control and dived off the road into a flooded ditch. Thorn quickly sped up to the SUV, stuck his gun out of the driver's side window, fired a full clip at the back window —tearing the window into pieces—and then sped off, hoping the bullets he had emptied into the SUV had managed to strike at least one of his targets.

Rita and Rhonda, as trained cops, immediately bent low in their seats and covered their heads when they heard the bullets start flying. Several of the bullets struck the front windshield, shattering it. The rest struck odd targets—but avoided Rita and Rhonda. "Talk to me!" Rita called out once the shooting eased up.

"I'm clear…you?" Rhonda yelled.

"I'm clear!"

Rhonda snatched off her seat belt as floodwaters began covering the floorboard, forced the passenger side door open, and waded out into waist-high flood water. All she saw were the taillights of the black SUV vanishing into the rain.

"I think we were warned," she called out as Rita crawled out of the SUV into the floodwaters with her gun at the ready.

Rita watched in misery at the taillights belonging to the black SUV faded away into the rain. "Thorn Bedford knows where Benita is, but thank goodness he's driving in the opposite direction," she yelled through the rain. "Grab our purses and let's get out of this flooded ditch." Rhonda nodded her head, returned to the SUV, retrieved two purses, and then joined Rita on the road. "I'm calling Billy—"

"No," Rita said in a quick voice. "Leave Billy at the farm with Benita."

Rita stared into Rhonda's eyes and then understood. "I'll call Brad."

"Good idea."

Rita put her gun away and called Brad, who was at home resting. When Rita described the event that had just taken place Brad exploded. "You girls hang tough. I'm on my way."

"With a tow truck," Rita told Brad.

"With a tow truck," Brad assured Rita and ended the call.

Rita put her cell phone back into her purse and then studied her flooded SUV. "Brad is on his way, sis. All we can do is wait."

Rhonda stared at the wrecked SUV. "Thorn Bedford could have stopped and finished us off. Why didn't he?"

"He did fire into the SUV," Rita pointed out as the heavy rain flooded down onto her tired and beautiful face. "Any of those bullets he fired into the SUV could have made contact."

"This was a warning, Rita," Rhonda insisted. "Next time we may not be so blessed." Rhonda turned her eyes away from the SUV, studied the rainy road, and then put her gun away. "Thorn Bedford is after Benita Cayberry because the woman has something he wants, and that something is—"

"Money," Rita finished as the heavy rain continued to fall from a dark, gray sky. "Sis, this case began in Los Angeles and has to end in Los Angeles."

Rhonda looked at Rita. "Are you suggesting a road trip?"

"Thorn Bedford is after Benita Cayberry. We need to take him—and Benita—back to California. I have a feeling that's the only location we're going to find the answers we're after." Rita patted Rhonda's shoulder. "I think Charlie knows this too."

"The nursing home?"

Rita nodded. "The nursing home," Rita said in a tired but confident voice. "In the meantime, we stand here in this rain…and wait."

"As the rain falls," Rhonda sighed, feeling as if she were trapped in a black-and-white 1950s detective book.

chapter seven

B illy wasn't too happy that Rita's SUV had been shot up by a crazed killer. Deep down he understood why the woman hadn't called him. Benita would have freaked out and might have attempted to run. Benita was already a bag of nerves waiting to explode—the last thing in the world Billy wanted to do was spook the little scarecrow. Of course, soaring through the air at over 500 mph probably wasn't helping. Flying on a commercial flight wasn't too bad for Billy, but Benita was ready to have a mental breakdown. "Will you try and relax," Billy told his panicked cousin. "We've just been in the air a little over half an hour."

Benita, who had an aisle seat, reached out and grabbed a flight attendant who looked meaner than snot. The flight attendant threw her eyes down at Benita and frowned. "Yes, Ms. Cayberry, what is it now?"

Charlie, who was sitting across from Benita, grinned and held a newspaper up to his face. Rita and Rhonda, who were sitting behind Benita, sunk down in their seats. "I felt a bump...are we crashing?" Benita asked with wide, bulging eyes.

"No, Ms. Cayberry, we're not crashing," the flight

attendant snapped, nearly biting Benita's head off. "What you felt was mild turbulence."

"She's just a little plane shy is all," Billy told the flight attendant, trying to sound pleasant. "My cousin doesn't like to fly."

"This is my first time…never again…never again!" Benita exclaimed, squeezing the flight attendant's arm.

The flight attendant took her right hand, peeled Benita's hand free, and rolled her eyes. "I'm sure the airlines will be most pleased to hear that news, Ms. Cayberry," she said in a sarcastic tone and strolled off.

"Will you calm down," Billy whispered in a stern tone. "Why, we have more of a chance of getting in a car accident… at least that's what I read."

"Car accidents kill a handful of people…planes…bunches all at once," Benita pointed out. She grabbed the arms of her seat and began taking deep breaths. "I can't believe I let you talk me into this, Cousin Billy."

"Look," Billy explained, "we drove all the way to Dallas and then hopped this flight in order to throw that fella who is chasing you off your scent. Now I know we just up and jumped ship yesterday without any warning, but Rita and Rhonda figured it was better to leave town the same day that fella ran them off into that flooded ditch rather than sit and wait around like a couple of dumb chickens."

"But going back to Los Angeles—"

"Maybe when we get to that city, you'll finally break and tell us why that fella named Debkins followed you to Clovedale Falls and why this fella Thorn is mighty determined to get you," Billy told Benita. "You didn't run from Los Angeles for no reason, gal."

Benita wasn't in the mood to talk anymore. Besides, what could she say? She ran because deep down inside of her heart she was afraid Mr. Agatha was going to kill her—or have Thorn kill her. Why? Because of that stupid Lloyd, that's why.

Lloyd and the sweet eyes he always made at Benita made Mr. Agatha believe she was involved in his crimes. And after Thorn went from being sweet to being downright threatening, Benita figured it was time to split. The only thing she couldn't understand was why Lloyd followed her to Clovedale Falls— or how the man even knew she was there.

What Benita didn't realize was that Lloyd and Thorn had decided to form a little…team in order to steal millions from Ron Agatha. However, Lloyd, assuming he was a clever man, decided to kill Thorn off…far away from Los Angeles. When Thorn informed Lloyd that Benita had put in for her vacation time and had bought a bus ticket, Lloyd saw a door of opportunity open to kill two birds with one stone. All Lloyd had to do was convince Thorn that Benita had stolen the bank codes from him—as he had been doing all along—and lure the man to Clovedale Falls, kill him, and then kill Benita. Of course, Thorn knew Lloyd was up to no good and pretended to go along with the plan…and killed Lloyd, but not before being duped into believing that Benita actually had the stolen bank codes.

And now Benita Cayberry, a hunted woman, was flying back to the same city she had fled from. "I must be crazy," she whispered.

Billy looked at Benita's crazy-colored hair—green, red, and yellow—and rolled his eyes. The woman's hair matched the crazy dress covering her Olive Oyl frame. "You are crazy," he promised.

"I don't mind being crazy, Cousin, just not so high up in the air," Benita said, feeling the tears well.

"Maybe we should have driven to Los Angeles," Rhonda whispered, taking a sip of soda sitting in a cold clear glass and then glancing around. "I know we're flying first class, but I feel like every passenger on this plane is ready to tear Benita apart."

"Thorn Bedford ran us off the road and filled my SUV full

of bullets, Rhonda," Rita whispered back, feeling a little uncomfortable in the fancy gray dress she was wearing. Pretending to be rich and wealthy wasn't exactly her gig. But the people—well, the eyes—waiting at the Los Angeles airport needed to see two wealthy women arriving with Benita. "Thorn trailed us all the way to Dallas, and then we lost him. Right now, that snake is probably shooting toward Los Angeles like a bullet, or maybe he hopped a plane. What matters is that we lost him…for the time being."

"I'm still not sure why you didn't want to face the creep," Rhonda said, feeling like a rich princess in the dark blue dress Billy had bought her on the way to Dallas. "I mean, sis, surely that creep has called ahead to Los Angeles—"

"To Mr. Agatha, yes, but not to Mrs. Owens," Rita pointed out. "Charlie made a call to Mrs. Owens for us." Rita leaned back in her seat, took a sip of cold soda, and tried to relax her mind. "Mrs. Owens and Mr. Agatha, according to Benita, were once in love. I'm depending on Mrs. Owens to put a net over Mr. Agatha and protect Benita."

"How does pretending to be rich and fancy play in?" Rhonda asked.

"Money," Rita explained, feeling a little turbulence make her stomach complain. "I'm certain Mr. Agatha knows we're cops—but we're retired, remember? We need to show up acting like a couple of fame-crazy gals who have some cash to spend while playing the good guys by returning Benita back to Mrs. Owens. We have to get Mr. Agatha on our good side…and lure Thorn Bedford into a trap. Once we deal with Thorn, we'll take Mr. Agatha down and get some real answers, since Benita has decided to clam up after finding out that Thorn Bedford tried to kill us."

Rhonda worked on her soda and then leaned her head out into the aisle, studied Charlie, and then sighed. "Charlie is really playing it cool."

"Charlie is a good guy."

Rhonda continued to look at Charlie. "You two came up with quite a plan. I wish I had been invited."

"Sis, the river was nearly up to our back door. You saved our home by spending all your time on the phone with that contractor. If that man hadn't shown up with that flood blockade when he did, we would have lost our cabin."

"That giant water tube around our cabin Mr. Lapsters put on...really neat how he did it," Rhonda said back in her seat. "It was good of Zach to foot the bill. That water tube wasn't cheap."

"Neither is our cabin," Rita pointed out, patting her sister's hand, and then took another sip of soda. "You saved our cabin while Charlie and I came up with a plan. It all works out together, sis."

Rhonda nodded her head toward Benita. "I'm wondering how that firecracker is going to work out," she whispered in a worried voice.

"We'll soon find out," Rita whispered back. "We have Brad trailing a day behind us. That man is our safety net. If the plan fails and we have to resort to gun play, Brad will show up in time. It was important to make Thorn think Brad stayed back in Clovedale Falls...and whoever else might have been watching—"

"If anyone else was watching," Rhonda whispered.

"I personally believe Thorn is acting alone," Rita whispered back. "What's important is that we shook him up. My guess is, and I could be wrong, Thorn Bedford was hoping to do two things: scare us away or kill us. When we tore out of town with Benita, I'm sure Thorn Bedford assumed we were running scared. But when we boarded our flight today for Los Angeles...I'm sure that snake isn't pleased."

"Shake up the can a little, right?"

"That's my hope," Rita agreed. "And it is also my hope to confuse Ron Agatha and make him turn on Thorn Bedford." Rita took another sip of soda. "Charlie isn't entirely confident if Benita is innocent or not. That's why he agreed to return Benita back to Mrs. Owens. Only time will tell."

"Only time will tell if your plan will work too," Rhonda told her sister in a troubled voice. "I'm sure Thorn Bedford isn't racing back to Los Angeles to hold our hands."

"I want Thorn Bedford to think Benita is crawling back to Mr. Agatha on her hands and knees." Rita finished off her soda. "We have to play as if we have never seen the man and don't even know who he is. Right now, we have absolutely no proof that he killed Mr. Debkins and, unfortunately, Brad didn't get a very good look at him either. If we're going to take Thorn Bedford down, we're going to have to play it smart and use Mr. Agatha as a pawn."

"I'm on board," Rhonda promised and then let her thoughts begin examining Rita's plan under a brighter light. Rita's plan had promise—but people were unpredictable. "Let's hope we're smarter than the average bear," Rhonda whispered. She closed her eyes and didn't open them until Los Angeles appeared under her feet.

"Okay, here we go," Rita said in a voice that sounded calm with just the slightest tremor of nervousness. She watched Billy stand up and help Benita unbuckle her seat belt, and then looked at Charlie. Charlie rose to his feet, shoved a cheap cigar in his mouth, fixed his fedora, and then nodded. "Charlie?" Rita said.

"I'll leave the plane first," Charlie told her. "I'll examine the area...causally...and then go outside and get a cab. Once I'm in the cab I'll call you. In the meantime, you four go directly to the food court and stay put. Don't leave the airport until I call you."

"This is like one of them old movies," Billy said in an

excited voice. "Boy, my life sure ain't boring no more. Ever since I met Rita and Rhonda, I've been on one crazy gig after another. Sure beats racking up cow poo."

Charlie smiled at Billy. "I'm sure it does," he agreed and then simply prepared to exit the plane.

"We'll wait a few minutes and let Charlie get ahead of us," Rita told everyone, allowing other first-class passengers to exit the plane.

Charlie wasn't a stupid man. He knew Mrs. Owens was going to be waiting at the airport along with Mr. Agatha. As much as he hated to throw Rita into a gutter—temporarily at least—Charlie did have a job to complete, a pay check to collect, and a killer to take down. Rita's plan would be carried out, but in time.

As smart as Rita and Rhonda were, Charlie feared they weren't capable of dealing with the big time. Thorn Bedford was big time. The man had a reputation and Charlie, who had bumped heads with Thorn in the past, wanted two things: revenge and closure. If he took down Thorn Bedford, his fading reputation would skyrocket, tons of work would appear, and he would no longer be living from one paycheck to another. Sure, the company Charlie worked for paid well, but as Charlie had told Rita and Rhonda earlier, his services were rarely required, forcing the man to stretch his pennies. Now Charlie had the chance to strike it big. Of course, he had to play it smart…real smart…while ensuring that he didn't lose the trust and friendship of three people he had come to call friends.

"Mrs. Owens should be…ah, yes," he said, walking into the crowded terminal and spotting Mrs. Owens standing off to the side with her cane. "Time to play." Charlie quickly approached Mrs. Owens while scanning the area for Mr. Agatha with skilled eyes. "Benita Cayberry is on the plane, Mrs. Owens."

Mrs. Owens stared at Charlie—stared at the man's fedora and wrinkled trench coat—and then focused on the terminal. "Where is she?" she asked.

Charlie folded his arms, examined the fancy pink dress Mrs. Owens was wearing, and offered a gentle smile. "You look like a vintage postcard, Mrs. Owens. Your appearance makes me miss the old days."

"I'm an old woman, Mr. Cook," Mrs. Owens told Charlie in a tired voice. "These trips are very tiresome. Please, let's step away from the pleasantries. I want my grandchild."

"Benita Cayberry will be exiting the plane shortly," Charlie promised as he causally glanced around. Ron Agatha was standing off in the distance, pretending to read a newspaper. "My job is complete. I brought your grandchild. Your job is to call my boss and report my success in order for me to get paid."

Mrs. Owens looked at Charlie. "Is my grandchild innocent?"

"Mrs. Owens," Charlie spoke in an innocent voice, "in today's time it's difficult to tell who is innocent and who isn't. All I can tell you is that Benita Cayberry, if she is guilty, is a victim of…circumstance." Charlie tipped his hat. "Good day, Mrs. Owens. Don't forget to call my boss." Charlie walked away just as Rita, Rhonda, Billy, and Benita exited the plane. Benita spotted Mrs. Owens and raised a grateful hand in the air.

"Oh…Benita, over here, child," Mrs. Owens called out, fighting back tears.

Benita pulled free from Billy, ran to Mr. Owens, and hugged the old woman. "Oh, what a terrible flight," she cried. "Oh, it's so good to be on the ground again…so good to see you." Mrs. Owens wrapped her tender arms around Benita and hugged the woman. Rita, Rhonda, and Billy watched—and so did Ron Agatha.

"They have arrived," Ron spoke into a cell phone. "I want them all dead—but only after I get my bank codes."

Thorn, who was on a late flight, nodded his head. "I understand," he said without telling Ron Agatha that the man was now on his hit list. What Thorn didn't know was that Brad was sitting two rows behind him.

"Mrs. Owens, this is my cousin Billy," Benita said, introducing a man wearing overalls and an old baseball cap to a fancy woman who understood diamonds and fame more than corn and pumpkins.

"Howdy, ma'am," Billy said and stuck out his right hand. "Mighty glad to meet you."

"Oh, Billy," Rita moaned under her breath as her cheeks turned red. Sure, Mrs. Owens was part of the case, but the woman was so lovely and delicate, and Billy was so…Billy.

Mrs. Owens, who was wearing a pair of white gloves, reached out, took the tip of Billy's fingers, and greeted him. "Likewise, I'm sure."

"And these two ladies are Rita and Rhonda Knight," Benita continued in a voice that was clearly thrilled to be back on solid ground. "Rita and Rhonda are retired cops and have been helping me—"

"Los Angeles!" Rita burst out in a silly voice that shocked everyone. "Oh, I can't believe I'm in Los Angeles. The fame… the celebrities…the movie studios…the mansions…the palm trees and bright sun…" Rita pretended to throw her eyes around in joy, spotting Ron Agatha in the process. "Oh, Rhonda, we have struck gold! We can finally use our inheritance the way we've always dreamed!"

Billy stared at Rita in complete shock. Had some cheesy actress with a goofy accent taken off with his bride-to-be?

Billy wasn't sure. "Uh…you feeling all right? Did you eat some bad peanuts on the plane?"

Rita nudged Billy in his rib with her elbow. "Forgive me, Mrs. Owens," she said in a voice loud enough for Ron to hear, "but you must understand that my sister and I have spent twenty long years fighting crime—twenty miserable years, I might add." Rita let out an overexaggerated sigh. "All my life I've dreamed of moving to Los Angeles and mingling with the stars…the sun…the palm trees. And now…look at me!"

Rhonda knew Rita's act—even though she was a bit shocked that her sister, Ms. Practical, had dived into the role of a goofy Valley Girl—and decided to join in…but not as dramatically. "We have sat on our inheritance for so long and now, all because of Benita…look at us!" Rhonda waved her arms around, spotted Ron, and continued on. "We have finally arrived, sis."

Rita nodded her head while throwing a quick glance at Ron. According to the photo that Brad had managed to pull, Ron Agatha was standing within hearing distance. "Let's go eat, okay? I want to have a full stomach when we start looking for a mansion to buy."

"A mansion?" Mrs. Owens asked, studying the twin sisters with confused eyes.

"A mansion?" Benita asked in a shocked voice, completely floored that Rita was acting so…impractical. Rita was the serious one and Rhonda was the funny one; at least from what Benita's crazy mind had been able to decipher. Now both sisters were acting nuts.

"Oh sure." Billy jumped into his part as easily as a dog carrying slippers into a den. "Rita and Rhonda have always wanted to live the big time…guess I have too." He grinned and then nudged Benita with his elbow and let out a chuckle. "Shoot, you didn't think we flew all this way just to drop you off and say bye, did you?"

"Well…no…." Benita looked at Billy with confused eyes.

What in the world was going on? First Rita and Rhonda had been drilling her for information and then…well, Rita and Rhonda had been run off the road Benita had to admit she had clammed up a bit. But so what? Who wouldn't clam up with a deadly killer on the loose? Clamming up under the weight of fear was normal. Rita and Rhonda's strange behavior wasn't.

"Look, girl," Rhonda said and patted Benita's arm, "we did all that we could to help you, so let us have some fun, huh? We brought you back to Los Angeles safe and sound, didn't we?"

"Well…yeah…."

"And you weren't the one killed, were you?" Rita asked, deciding to throw Ron for a loop.

"No."

"Killed?" Mrs. Owens asked in a shocked voice.

"Yeah," Rita said matter-of-factly, as if the mention of murder was no big deal, "some guy named Lloyd Debkins ate a bullet. But don't worry, we cleared Benita of all wrongdoing. Too bad we didn't catch the killer."

"Killers always give cops a hard time," Rhonda added, "but as you can see, we always bounce back. And sometimes a killer just…slips through our hands. Now, where's the food court, huh? I'm starved."

"Uh…that way, I believe," Mrs. Owens stated and pointed a shaky finger over her shoulder.

"Great." Rita beamed. "We'll eat and then go look at all those beautiful mansions."

Rhonda decided to really throw a cherry onto the cake. "But what if we don't have enough money, sis?" she frowned. "Our inheritance—"

"Button your lip," Rita snapped in a quick voice and pointed to a man who was standing a few feet away talking on a cell phone. "We don't need to advertise that we have millions," she whispered. "Now come on, let's go eat." Rita grabbed Benita's hand and pulled the woman away from Mrs. Owens.

"Let's eat." Billy smiled at Mrs. Owens, took the woman's arm, and carefully walked away with her, leaving Ron feeling confused.

Ron watched Rita and Rhonda walk away with Benita, tossed his newspaper into a nearby trashcan, and then slowly began to follow. Rita had mentioned millions. "Who are these women?" Ron asked himself, walking through the crowded airport toward the food courts. "Could they be an answer to this old man's problem?" Ron wasn't sure. All he knew was that Lloyd Debkins was dead, Benita Cayberry was back in Los Angeles, and two strange women and a hillbilly-type character had arrived with her. "Retired cops who have money to spend…," Ron whispered as his mind struggled to set apart facts from suspicion.

Rita pretended to trip, grabbed ahold of Rhonda, and rubbed her ankle. "Ron Agatha is following us," she whispered in Rhonda's ear. "We have to reel him in so follow my lead."

"You got it," Rhonda whispered back.

Rita let go of Rhonda and looked at Billy. "Silly me…these heels aren't agreeing with me."

"Of…course," Mrs. Owens said. "Heels can be difficult at times, I suppose."

Rita smiled. "I'm sure not going mansion hunting in these heels," she claimed. "I'll stop and buy me a pair of walking shoes."

"Yes, uh, shouldn't we go retrieve your luggage before—" Mrs. Owens began to ask.

"No luggage." Rita beamed. "We're buying everything new. Only our purses," Rita patted her purse, "and Billy's wallet. Nothing more for this group."

"We want to buy Los Angeles clothes and look all fancy."

Billy snickered. "I might buy a pair of overalls that shines and sparkles and a pair of them dark sunglasses."

"Of course," Mrs. Owens told Billy, not certain how to respond. "Benita, darling, perhaps you and I should return to the home and let your...friends...continue on without us? I am quite tired."

"No can do," Billy exclaimed, letting go of Mrs. Owens's arm and walking over to Benita. "My cousin ain't leaving my eyesight. No, ma'am. Not after all the trouble she's been through." Billy took Benita's arm. "This here gal is family and I ain't leaving her side until I'm as confident as a mule eating corn that's she okay. Besides, it's been a dry spell since we last saw each other and we have some lost times to catch up on, yes sir."

"I...see." Mrs. Owens frowned. "Well...Benita, I was hoping we could have dinner at the home tonight. Just the two of us. You worried me so when you disappeared without saying goodbye. And...it does seem like there has been some form of trouble. I would like very much for you to—"

"Oh sure, we'll all have supper tonight," Billy cut Mrs. Owens off. "Benita has told us all about the nursing home she worked at." Billy looked at Rita and Rhonda. "What say... around seven o'clock?"

"Seven sounds good to me," Rita said.

"Seven isn't a problem." Rhonda smiled. "Benita?"

Benita looked at Rita, Rhonda, and Billy like they were all nuts. "Uh...sure...I guess."

"Seven it is, then," Mrs. Owens stated. She threw a desperate eye at Benita. "My poor dear, I'm very sorry that you have experienced tragedy, but I'm very grateful that you are home." Mrs. Owens walked over to Benita and offered a gentle hug. "Please, come by the home for dinner tonight... and if needed, yes, bring your friends."

"I'll be there," Benita promised in an uneasy voice. "Uh... will Mr. Agatha be at the home?"

"I'm not quite sure," Mrs. Owens answered, fully aware that the man she had once loved was standing close by. "My dear, as I told you once before, Mr. Agatha has no ill will toward you."

"So you say," Benita replied, looking nervous. "That man scares me."

Mrs. Owens patted Benita's hand. "No need to worry about Ron Agatha," she promised Benita. "Ron is harmless. Now, enough talk. I'll see you at seven." Mrs. Owens offered Benita a loving smile and then walked away into the busy airport, vanishing among the rush of travelers.

Rita stood still until Mrs. Owens vanished and then waited for Mr. Agatha to follow. Like clockwork the old man swam past her in a crowd of people and vanished. "There he goes." Rita nodded her head at Ron. "We better get to the food court."

"Will someone tell me what's going on?" Benita demanded. "I know I ain't the smartest fish in the tank, but I do know you just threw pie in the face of that sweet old woman."

Rita turned to Benita with stern eyes. "We're saving your life and capturing a killer at the same time," she explained. "The information you've supplied up until this point has been helpful, Benita, but not damaging. But that's all right because we have a plan in place. All you have to do is play along."

"Well, why didn't you tell me, for crying out loud?" Benita exclaimed. "I'm part of your team too."

"We didn't tell you, gal," Billy told Benita, "because these two ladies wanted to see how your mouth and eyes acted with that old lady."

"We also needed to see how Mr. Agatha was going to react as well," Rita explained.

"Mr. Agatha…was here?" Benita gulped.

Rita sighed. "Benita, the man just walked past you. Oh, never mind."

Rhonda fought back a grin. "Come on, let's go to the food court and wait for Charlie to call us."

Outside the airport Charlie had a cab begin making circles. The cabbie, a seventy-four-year-old retired baseball player, had nothing better to do. Besides, he knew Charlie and didn't mind offering a helping hand. "Anything?"

Charlie was about to say no when he spotted Mrs. Owens step out of the airport and get into a black limousine. A few minutes later Ron joined her. "Wait a few minutes," Charlie told his friend. "We need to see if anybody else comes out." When the limousine drove away Charlie nodded his head. "Follow—"

"Yeah, I know, Charlie," the cabbie barked. "I've been around long enough to know my part."

Charlie grinned as the cabbie took off and then called Rita. "Mrs. Owens and Ron Agatha left in a limousine together. I'm following them. Rent an SUV and take your team and meet me at 9997 Dry Dust Lane. Don't park. We'll wait for Thorn Bedford to show up together.

"Understood," Rita assured Charlie. "Want us to bring any food?" Rita spotted a Chick-Fil-A and saw Billy's eyes light up. "I think Billy is hungry."

"Food would be nice," Charlie told Rita as he chewed on a cheap cigar.

"You got it."

Charlie nodded his head, ended the call, and told the cabbie to stay close. "This traffic—"

"Rush hour traffic, what do you expect?" the cabbie fussed. "I've lived in LA since the day I was born and each year the city gets worse and worse. Mostly it's those stupid kids who don't know how to drive!" The cabbie dashed out onto a busy highway and began swerving between a variety of vehicles. "Get out of my way, you punks!"

Charlie leaned back in his seat and, feeling like he was back in the old days, folded his arms together and watched his friend fight his way through the congested traffic. "If I do this right, I'll dig my name out of the grave," he whispered. "I can take down Thorn Bedford and see what no-good activity Ron Agatha was dipping his hands in. This case could be what brings my career back to life."

Far ahead, the limo Mrs. Owens and Ron Agatha were in carefully moved through the traffic. "Ron," Mrs. Owens said in a troubled voice, savoring the cold air hitting her face, "I'm worried for Benita."

"Don't be worried," Ron promised. "Lilly, you heard those two women…millions. This could be my big chance to save my life, the home, and buy the studio." Ron reached out and took Mrs. Owens's hand. "Lilly, there are no more chances. If Benita truly doesn't have my bank codes…if Lloyd did pull a fast one on Thorn…then there is no chance for any of us."

"Benita is innocent," Mrs. Owens insisted in a strained voice. "Ron, my grandchild is innocent. I can see her sweet eyes. Yes, she is…different…but she is not guilty of theft or… murder." Mrs. Owens turned away from Ron. "I…how will you get the money?" she asked in a miserable voice.

"Thorn Bedford is flying into LA later today," Ron explained in a careful voice. "I'm going to use him to blackmail Benita's two friends."

"Use?" Mrs. Owens asked in a confused voice.

Ron slowly folded his arms. "Kill," he confessed. "Thorn Bedford has to die and I plan to use his death to force Benita's friends to give me their money…or else."

Mrs. Owens turned her head and looked into Ron's determined eyes. "There really is no chance to locate the stolen bank codes?" she asked in a miserable voice.

"Lloyd Debkins is dead. Thorn believes Benita has the codes. You believe the woman is innocent," Ron answered. "Lilly, at this point I can't rely on locating my stolen bank codes any longer. I must move into a different studio and write a different script."

"Yes, I suppose," Mrs. Owens sighed as her heart broke. "For the sake of Benita...and the home."

Ron unfolded his arm, took Mrs. Owens's hand, and nodded. "Everything is going to end well, Lilly. I promise."

Mrs. Owens wasn't so certain. Murder never ended well... not even in the movies.

chapter eight

The Green Mansion Nursing Home sat up in the canyons that overlooked Los Angeles. The home, sitting on twenty acres of dry, parched land, had been an old mansion built by an eccentric writer in 1887. Over the years the mansion had changed ownership, being transformed into everything from a private home to an art gallery, finally ending up in the hands of Ron Agatha, who turned the mansion into a nursing home for the rich and famous. The mansion was, in itself, very spooky in appearance, resembling a place designed to hold a morgue rather than people. The inside of the mansion, however, was absolutely gorgeous—a true place for the rich and famous and spoiled living.

"Goodness," Rhonda said, driving past the mansion in a green Dodge Journey.

"Don't let the land fool you," Benita called out from the back seat, straining her eyes through a tall black iron gate in order to see the mansion. "The grounds in back have been turned into some awful pretty flower gardens. Sure takes a lot of water to keep those gardens looking pretty too."

"Looks like a funeral home," Billy said in a creepy voice. "Why would someone want to live in that thing?"

Rita stuck her head over the front seat and looked at Billy. "I guess this is how the rich live."

"The rich don't have no sense," Billy fussed.

"Hey," Benita objected, "that home is mighty pretty inside. So what if the outside looks a little gray and rainy and all. The inside is enough to rock your socks."

Billy shook his head. "My socks are just fine at home, thank you."

Rita grinned, turned back around, and studied the dry street the SUV was climbing. "Charlie should be around here someplace, sis."

"Maybe he's farther up the road." Rhonda stepped on the gas and forced the SUV to climb higher up into the canyons, driving around one dangerous curve after another, riding past fancy homes sitting on dry, parched land. "Hey, there he is!"

Rita looked to where Rhonda had pointed her eyes, saw Charlie standing outside of a run-down taxi, and nodded. "Yes, that is Charlie. I wonder why he decided to meet us so far up."

Charlie spotted a green SUV approaching and immediately knew it was his friends. "Okay, old friend, here's your money—"

"Oh, keep your money, Charlie," the cabbie fussed. "I don't drive this cab for money and you know it. I have enough cash in the bank to run me until the Lord calls me home. I drive this cab because I'm a bored old man who likes to sit out by the airport and watch the planes land."

Charlie stuck his head down next to the driver's side window and looked at his friend. "You miss the old days?" he asked.

"You bet I do," the cabbie confessed and then simply let out a sad sigh. "Men our age can only look back, Charlie, because this world don't want us anymore." With those words the cabbie made a sharp U-turn, barely missing the green SUV Rhonda was driving by a mere inch, and headed back down the canyon.

"Take care, old friend," Charlie whispered. He shoved a cheap cigar into his mouth and then began to hum an old Christian hymn as Rhonda and Rita climbed out of the SUV.

"Why are you so far up?" Rhonda asked as the hot sun sitting in the clear blue sky began beating down on her hair. The sun was not summer hot but hot enough to cause a woman to break a sweat.

"The home is eaten alive with security cameras," Charlie explained. "It's better if we stay out of sight." Charlie walked over to the green SUV, leaned against the hood, and folded his arms. "Okay, ladies, here's where old Charlie sets some rules." Rita and Rhonda looked at each with nervous eyes. "I need to dig my name out of the grave it's sitting in, and in order to do that I need a big job…like this one." Charlie inclined his head toward the right side of the road. It was wide open, offering a clear view of downtown LA. "That's a tough town. If I'm going to make it, I need to score big."

"Charlie—" Rita began.

Charlie held up a hand while keeping his eyes hidden under the fedora stationed on his head. "Thorn Bedford and I have a score to settle," he continued. "Years back Thorn almost killed me. I know quite a few people would like to see the guy swimming with the fish…including me. But before I put him in his place, I'm going to make him tell me what no good crimes Ron Agatha has his fingers in." Charlie paused, chewed on his cigar, and then continued. "Rita, we'll continue with your plan. I think if we play our cards right, Ron Agatha might take the bait—only if we can make him believe Benita is innocent. In the meantime, I'm certain Thorn will show up…." Charlie paused again, chewed on his cigar, and then nodded his head. "From this point forward, no one is alone. We work in pairs, including me." Charlie pointed toward the back passenger seat. "Billy," he called out, "you're with me.

Rita and Rhonda will work as a team. Benita, you're with Mrs. Owens."

"I guess that's my cue," Billy told Benita and then locked eyes with the scared woman. "Now listen here, gal. You do as Charlie Cook tells you. We're here to make sense of this mess and clean it up—"

"Billy, I'm not in cahoots with Lloyd Debkins," Benita said, cutting Billy off. "You have to believe me. I ran because I was afraid Mr. Agatha figured I *was* in cahoots...and when Thorn turned mean, I knew it was time to get out of town." Benita grabbed Billy's hand. "I don't know why Lloyd followed me to Clovedale Falls...honest. I've said all I know...in my own way. I mean...my mind doesn't have all the facts straightened out because I sure don't know why Lloyd followed me to Clovedale Falls. I sure do know that Thorn thinks I have a piece of gold...and if he does...Mr. Agatha will too." Benita looked down at her shaky hands. "I'll go back to the home tonight and I'll stay close to Mrs. Owens—only because I trust you. I guess if I end up dead and all...well, that's just the way it'll have to be, huh?"

Billy felt his heart break. "Listen, gal," he said in a tender voice, "ain't no one gonna hurt my cousin as long as Billy Northfield has air in his lungs, you hear? I admit this case has some sharp corners, but it ain't all that hard to figure out, right? Sure. What we have is a man who found another man was doing some bad things, stole that man's toys...and in return the other man hired a bad guy to fetch his toys back. And somehow you got caught up in the mess. Sound about right?"

"I...uh...guess?" Benita made a pained face. "The only problem is everyone thinks I have the toy Lloyd stole and I don't."

Billy scratched the back of his neck. "Well, that fellow followed you to Clovedale Falls for a reason. I reckon we'll find out what the reason was sooner or later." Billy offered

Benita a strong smile, crawled out into the hot sun with his overalls just a-beaming, and walked over to Charlie. "I reckon we're a team."

Charlie gave a brief nod. "Our job is to sneak into the home and stay out of sight," he explained. "Tonight, when Rita and Rhonda attend dinner, one of them will let us in."

"Hey, this is just like in the movies." Billy beamed proudly and then leaned back next to Charlie. "What about all of this, huh?" he said as the hot sun washed down onto his farm-stained face. "Old Billy Northfield is in the big city solving a big crime. I reckon if this don't impress your folks," he told Rita, "nothing will."

Rita stared at Billy's overalls. A backwoods farmer wearing overalls while solving crimes. Oh yeah, that was surely going to impress her parents. "Maybe if you were wearing a tuxedo...honey?"

"Aw," Billy said, throwing his hand at Rita, "there ain't a thing in the world wrong with a man's overalls. Overalls gives a man space to work and think."

Charlie grinned. Billy Northfield sure was a character. "While we wait for dinnertime to arrive," he told Rita and Rhonda, "I want you girls to drive back to the airport and wait for Thorn to arrive. If you don't see him at least half an hour before dinnertime, leave the airport and get back to the home. Traffic will be difficult and you'll need a good half hour for driving time."

"And if we do spot Thorn?" Rita asked, assuming Brad—who, even though he had barely gotten a decent look at Thorn's face, was certain he was on the trail of the right man —wouldn't be far behind. "Then what?"

"Call me and then tail him," Charlie explained. "You two ladies know your stuff and there's plenty of traffic to disguise yourself in. It's my guess that when Thorn Bedford arrives back in LA, he'll go straight to the home." Charlie checked the cheap watch he was wearing. "We have a few hours...you girls get back to the airport. Billy and I are going to sit tight right here." Charlie pointed at a pale green bungalow located down a concrete driveway. "We'll be in there," he explained. "The bungalow is up for sale and will be a good place to wait." Charlie removed the cheap cigar from his mouth. "I wish I had my car and all those neat toys my company gave me. Looks like I'm playing it the old way."

Charlie walked back to Benita and opened her car door. "Ms. Cayberry," he spoke in a polite but stern tone, "no games. My gut is telling me you might be innocent. Don't make me regret that feeling. All you need to do is stay beside Mrs. Owens."

"Sure," Benita promised. "Mrs. Owens and I are really good friends."

"Maybe more than that." Charlie smiled, leaving Benita confused. "Okay, Billy," he called out, "let's get out of this sun for a while."

"You know where I'm at," Billy told Rita. He kissed her cheek and then wandered away with Charlie at his side.

Rita touched her cheek and then climbed back into the SUV. Rhonda waited until Charlie and Billy reached the front door of the bungalow before jumping into the driver's seat. "Benita, honey, you're with us until dinnertime."

"Oh, I don't mind," Benita told Rhonda as the SUV conducted a sharp U-turn, barely missing the edge of the road. "You gals have been really nice to me…reckon it ain't been easy. I mean…well, I am a bit crazy, huh?" Benita touched her funny-colored hair. "I just figured since the world didn't want me, I'd be as crazy as I felt."

"Honey…," Rita began but then stopped. What could she say to Benita that would be beneficial? "It doesn't matter what the world thinks," she finally said as Rhonda drove past the mansion again. "My parents raised Rhonda and me on one solid principle."

"What's that?"

"Stay inside the boundaries of the Bible and never care what the world thinks," Rita explained, throwing her eyes off the canyon hills and letting them fall on Los Angeles. "Rita and I became cops because we believed in justice. Justice is rejected in a city like Los Angeles. LA is consumed with crime, greed, corruption, and egos. Everyone wants to be a movie star or a famous singer. Movie studios swallow people's very souls, turning them into puppets." Rita pointed out the window. "While the city may appear attractive and even beautiful, underneath it all lies a filth that some people will never be able to wash off." Rita lowered her finger. "Benita, honey, it's not what the world thinks of you...it's what you think of yourself and do for yourself that you know and feel is right."

"I've never known what was right for me," Benita confessed in a sad voice. "I've always been such a goofball... such an oddball. It wasn't until I began working at the home...until I met Mrs. Owens that I seemed to... well, you know, find my place. But boy, that sure didn't work out. Stupid Lloyd messed it all up...giving me sweet eyes. I mean, for real, can you imagine a gal like me going for a grandpa? Yuck." Benita shook her hands into the air like she was trying to shake dirt off her hands. "A woman has her pride. Well, I did until Thorn began smiling at me. But he turned out to be a fake." Benita sighed. "Now I'm just lost all over again. I reckon Cousin Billy will teach me a trade or something."

Rita desperately wanted to tell Benita that Mrs. Owens was her grandmother but didn't. She knew it wasn't her place to reveal such a shocking revelation. Benita was going to have to find out on her own. Until then, she had business to tend to. "Rhonda—" Rita's cell phone cut her off. "It's Brad," Rita said, checking the call.

"He couldn't have landed in Los Angeles so soon?" Rhonda asked.

Rita shrugged her shoulders. "Brad?"

"I've just landed at LAX," Brad said in a quick voice. "Thorn Bedford is making his way outside."

Rita checked her watch and was shocked to see that over two hours had passed since they'd landed. The traffic had been horrible…but two hours? "Rhonda and I are on our way to the airport—"

"Cancel that," Brad ordered. "I managed to hear Thorn talking on his cell phone. He's taking a cab and going directly to the Green Mansion Nursing Home. I won't be far behind him."

Rhonda let off the gas and hit the brakes. "Looks like we're turning around."

Rita nodded her head. "Brad, have a cab bring you to 9997 Dry Dust Lane. It's a little green bungalow that sits up the road from the nursing home. We'll be there with Benita, Billy, and Charlie."

"Will do," Brad said, stepping outside of the airport into the hot sun. "I want this guy taken down, Rita. He's mine."

"Charlie might object to that," Rita said as Rhonda made another sharp U-turn and began racing back up the canyon road. "Look, Brad, just grab a cab. Remember 9997 Dry Dust Lane—and be careful, okay? You may be grouchy lately but you're our grouch and we care about you."

Brad watched Thorn jump into a cab and speed off. "I'm on my way," he promised and then added, "Thanks for caring."

"Anytime." Rita smiled as Rhonda zoomed past the home. "You know us cops…always in a mess…and always sticking together," she said as the hot sun beat down on the canyon, turning the dry land into a mysterious riddle.

Seven o'clock arrived. Rita and Rhonda slowly pulled up to the front gate sitting in front of the mansion with Benita. "Play it smart," Rita whispered.

Rhonda nodded her head, stuck her right hand out of the window, and pressed a black button connected to a security box. "Yes?" a woman's voice asked as a red light attached to a security camera studying the green SUV began to glow.

"My name is Rhonda Knight. I'm here to have dinner with Mrs. Owens...Benita Cayberry and my sister, Rita Knight, are with me," Rhonda called out as if she were speaking into a drive-through menu speaker, deliberately acting dumb. Rita and Rhonda agreed that they needed to make people in California believe people from Georgia were mighty dumb.

"Yes, you are expected," the woman spoke to Rhonda in a bored voice followed by a loud *buzz*. The black iron gate made a loud *click* and slowly began to ease open.

"That was Ellie. She's kinda of a drag," Benita explained, leaning forward on her elbows. "She's sixty years old, never been married, and kinda bitter. I never liked her much...acts too much like a sour goat."

Rhonda rolled her eyes as she pulled through the gate and listened to Benita chew on and on about Ellie. By the time she parked next to a fancy blue BMW, she felt like her ears might fall off. "Anyways," Benita finished, "we'll stay clear of Ellie. She's in the front office anyway, so I doubt she'll be a bother."

"Let's hope," Rita said, bending down and checking the gun attached to her ankle. Charlie had made a call, and as promised, managed to get some guns back into the scene. An old man who looked real mean delivered a load of guns to the bungalow Charlie had decided to take cover in—and just in time for dinner too. Rita knew Charlie would come through but boy did he cut it close. "Okay, we stay together as a team...and Benita...honey, just play along, okay?"

"Oh sure, you bet...absolutely...with all my heart and all that jazz," Benita promised. "You know me. Old Benita can play any song and play along, yes sir. Old Benita is your woman and—"

"We get it, honey," Rhonda sighed, turning in her seat and focusing on Benita. Benita was so very sweet and innocent—a blabbermouth who didn't know when to shut up—but sweet and innocent. "You're okay, Benita." Rhonda smiled. "A little…different…but I'd rather have a million of you than a so-called normal person any day."

"Really?" Benita asked in a shocked voice. "Even though I kinda insulted the way Rita makes coffee?"

Rita turned to face Benita. "You're a gentle soul, Benita… and while you may have a mouth, well, it's like my sister just told you. We would rather have a million of you than a so-called normal person any day. Why? Because your heart is like gold."

"Aw…shucks." Benita blushed. "I ain't nothing special."

"You are to us." Rhonda patted Benita's hand and then pointed at the mansion. "Now, we need to be at our best, okay?"

"You bet!" Benita said, feeling all fired up. Rita and Rhonda liked her—they really liked her. Wow, she had real, actual friends that didn't live on the pages of a comic book. "I'm your gal, yes sir!"

Rhonda smiled at Rita. "She's our gal," she said. She climbed out of the SUV, stretched her arms, and then studied the other vehicles parked in the small parking lot sitting on the east side of the mansion: a limo, a few fancy BMWs—all BMWs…figured. "It'll be dark soon." Rita waited for Rhonda to join her before making a move. "Okay, sis, Thorn is inside and we can be pretty certain that he's with Ron Agatha, waiting for us."

"Charlie, Billy, and Brad will move into position in thirty minutes. Our job is to disable the security system and unlock the back door," Rhonda whispered as Benita crawled out of the backseat. "We won't have much time to take Thorn down—"

"We have to play Ron Agatha just right...for Benita's sake," Rita whispered. "Thorn is our target tonight. Ron Agatha will be our future target. Tonight, we'll just bait the guy while Thorn is taken out of the picture."

"That's the plan," Rhonda said. She checked the fancy blue dress she was wearing and drew in a deep breath. "Let's play ball."

Rita reached out and took Benita's hand. "Oh, this is so fancy...wow," she exclaimed. "I can't wait to get inside!"

Thorn locked his eyes on a security screen and watched Benita hurry Rita and Rhonda around to the front door of the mansion. "I ran them off the road and filled the SUV they were in full of bullets. This is a trap," he warned Ron.

Ron watched Benita arrive at the front door. Rita and Rhonda were not acting like two women who had been targeted by a killer. The actions and attitudes of the two women made Ron worry that Thorn was lying—and that's exactly the effect Rita and Rhonda desired.

"I'll handle the two cops," he warned Thorn. "You stay out of sight."

Thorn kept his eyes on the security screen perched on Ron's desk. Benita was so close—Thorn could taste the millions Lloyd had stolen. There were too many people present, however, to simply shoot his way through to Benita, too many witnesses. He had to play it smart. *I'll wait until dinner begins, kill the old man, and then go for Benita,* Thorn thought to himself as Maye Welsh, a seventy-year-old house cleaner, pulled open a large wooden front door and greeted Benita.

Ron glanced at Thorn, saw evil radiating in the man's eyes, and clearly understood what plans were being formed. Thorn had to die—and fast. But first Ron knew he had to ensure that Rita and Rhonda were indeed...loaded. It was time to outsmart the fox. "Thorn, remain in my office. I will return in one hour."

"Fine," Thorn growled under his breath. He sat down on the edge of Ron's desk, folded his arms, and continued to study the security screen.

Ron checked the gray suit he was wearing—a gray suit that looked similar to the suit Thorn had decided to don—walked out of his office, moved down a long, beautiful hallway, and found Rita, Rhonda, and Benita standing in a spacious foyer greeting Mrs. Owens.

"Ah, the guests have arrived," he said in a pleasant tone that gave Benita the creeps. "Benita, back from your vacation so soon?"

Benita flinched. Ron Agatha terrified her. Something about the man—something deep down—was so evil and hideous; it was like the man's heart was covered with a black ooze that had killed whatever decency had once struggled to find life. "Uh...yes, sure," Benita said in a quick voice. "You know me...uh...anxious to get back to work."

"Of course." Ron smiled and then turned his attention to Rita and Rhonda. "My, you two are a pleasant sight to this old man's eyes." Ron widened his smile. "Welcome to the Green Mansion Nursing Home. My name is Mr. Agatha. I'm the owner. And of course, I believe you know Mrs. Lilly Owens."

"We met at the airport," Mrs. Owens informed Ron, disappointed that Benita had arrived with guests.

"We sure did." Rita beamed and then began to admire the spacious foyer like a silly schoolgirl. "My, what a place. Look at all this fancy wood. And the carvings...owls...goodness."

"And look at this carpet," Rhonda exclaimed. "It's all red."

"The color is mahogany," Ron informed Rhonda as he studied the woman with skilled eyes disguised as a tired old man who was attempting to act as a pleasant host. "Please, ladies, follow me into the main dining hall."

"I thought we would have tea in the sitting room first," Mrs. Owens told Ron. "I had Mitch place a fire in the fireplace."

"Of course." Ron smiled at Mrs. Owens. "I'll have Maye serve four glasses of the orange spice tea you enjoy so much."

"I'd rather have the apple cinnamon tea if that's okay. I mean…I can have orange spice—" Benita began to stumble all over herself.

Ron smiled. "Apple cinnamon for Benita," he promised. "Ladies, what's your preference?"

"Oh, good old-fashioned sweet tea," Rita exclaimed, hoping to sound like Billy. Of course, only Billy could talk about southern sweet tea the right way—Billy had a talent for making sweet tea sound like gold. "The sweeter the better."

"And bunches of ice," Rhonda added and smiled at Mrs. Owens. "Tea ain't tea without ice."

"I…suppose," Mrs. Owens replied and quickly took Benita's hand. "Why don't you ladies allow Ron to give you a tour. Benita and I will be in the sitting room."

"No can do," Rhonda said and grabbed Benita's other hand. "We promised Billy we wouldn't let this little pony out of our sight."

Benita looked at Mrs. Owens. "My cousin Billy…worries," she struggled to explain.

"And he should," Rita pointed out and looked at Ron with eye that she hoped were very serious but a bit…'Gooberish,' as Rhonda always said. "One of your employees was found dead in Clovedale Falls, Georgia, Mr. Agatha. That's serious business. But don't worry…about an hour ago or so—"

"Forty-one minutes to be exact, sis," Rhonda stated and then rolled her eyes. "You always get the time wrong—"

"Do not," Rita barked at Rhonda.

"You do too, darn it," Rhonda barked back, hoping to sound as hillbilly as possible and then turned her attention to Ron. "Twenty years we worked as cops in Atlanta and not once...not one time...did my sister ever get the time right. Every report she wrote was—"

"Are you still going to crawl down my spine because I got a few seconds off?" Rita asked, throwing her hands up into the air and rolling her eyes. "You're impossible. It's a wonder why Daddy left you half my share of the inheritance."

"Half your share?" Rhonda exploded. "Why, Daddy left you half my share!"

"That's a laugh!" Rita fired back and then grabbed Ron's hand. "Anyway," she said, pretending to ignore Rhonda, "our good doctor friend called and said he believes your employee, this Mr. Debkins, probably killed himself and wasn't murdered after all...something about the angle of the bullet?"

"We're retired, you see," Rhonda told Ron and shot Rita a sour look, "so we don't take cases as serious anymore. I mean, no offense, but cops get paid pennies. My sister and I did our time for twenty years, so why should we waste our time worrying about some lovesick hound dog that was stalking poor Benita?"

"Besides," Rita added, "even if Mr. Debkins was killed, so what? We did all we could do...forensics and all that stuff."

Rhonda reached out and patted Benita's shoulder. "Our real job was to get Benita back home safe and sound. Whoever killed Mr. Debkins, assuming it was murder and not a suicide, probably got what he wanted and split."

"Our professional guess is," Rhonda told Ron, "that Mr. Debkins was planning to kidnap Benita and run...and if he was killed—which we originally suspected was the cause of death—then he was probably mixed in with some bad folks who caught up to him. It happens."

"My sister believes the killer made Mr. Debkins's murder look like a suicide," Rita told Ron.

"Wouldn't be the first time!" Rhonda fired at Rita.

"Wouldn't be the first time you were wrong either. Remember the Wallace case? Huh? Remember?"

Rhonda was impressed her twin sister was pulling off a very convincing act—an act Ron Agatha was buying.

"Look, all I'm saying is that the killer could have—"

"Please," Mrs. Owens begged, "enough. What matters is that Benita is back home safe and sound."

"Of course," Ron said, pretending to sound shocked. "I... was unaware of these events," he lied. "I...fired Lloyd Debkins after I realized he was stealing from me. I never assumed—my goodness."

"Aw, don't go getting all upset," Rita told Ron. "My sister and me have seen it all. Murder is murder. Now, what about that tea, huh?" she asked as her eyes searched around for security cameras. To her relief Rita spotted security cameras sitting in expected locations. "Benita, you might as well come to the kitchen with us."

"I guess I better," Benita apologized to Mrs. Owens.

"I'll accompany you, then," Mrs. Owens informed Benita. "I do worry about you so."

"I think I will return to my office," Ron said. "I am quite shaken up by this news and need to sit down. Maye will tend to the tea." Ron began to walk off and then paused. It was time to throw a hook at Rita and Rhonda. "Money seems to be the bait for all murder, doesn't it? I would be careful with your inheritance, especially in LA."

"Shoot," Rita said in a quick voice, "my sister and I are planning to take our inheritance and become famous. All we gotta do is meet the right people, right, sis?"

"You bet," Rhonda claimed and then offered Ron a curious smile. "Say, you wouldn't happen to know any movie people, would you?"

Ron glanced at Mrs. Owens. Mrs. Owens looked down at the expensive carpet. "Under the circumstances I believe it wouldn't be proper to talk about such matters—out of respect for Mr. Debkins. But in time, if you ladies remain in town, perhaps I can introduce you to some people I know."

Rita and Rhonda began clapping their hands like silly schoolgirls. "Did you hear that!" Rita exclaimed. "We're going to be famous...and we have all of Daddy's money to help us!"

"Now we can throw our lousy pensions into the toilet and really start living!" Rhonda clapped her hands. "Oh, Mr. Agatha, you're our hero!"

"Well, I may know a few people in the business." Ron smiled and walked away. As soon as he was out of sight, he hurried back toward his office. "Thorn Bedford had not been telling me the truth. Those two stupid women aren't acting a bit scared...not like two women who were run off the road and shot at. No...Thorn has been lying to me. He has to die."

Ron stopped in front of his office door, removed an old six-shooter from his jacket pocket, and turned into a hungry snake that was prepared to strike. Thorn, who was sitting on the other side of the office door, had no idea he was about to die. Why? Because Thorn believed Ron was an old, washed-out man who didn't have the guts to step on an ant let alone go toe to toe with a deadly killer.

Thorn was wrong.

chapter nine

R ita followed Mrs. Owens into a large kitchen made of gray stone and a luxurious blue tile floor that complemented rows and rows of stainless-steel appliances. The kitchen was enough to melt any woman's heart. However, Rita was more fascinated with the back door.

"The back door," she whispered to Rhonda. "I'll unlock it somehow, and you pretend you need to use the bathroom and go call Charlie."

"Got it," Rhonda whispered, watching Maye exit a long pantry carrying an armload of teas. The poor woman, who was dressed in a long, 1920s black maid's uniform, appeared absolutely exhausted. Rhonda felt sorry for her, but sadly, Maye chose to work long hours simply because she was lonely. "Uh…Maye?" she asked.

"Yes?" Maye asked, setting down all the teas she had retrieved from the old pantry onto a long kitchen counter covered with expensive Spanish white tile.

"I need to use the little ladies' room? Too much coffee, you understand." Rhonda blushed.

Maye looked at Mrs. Owens. Mrs. Owens nodded. "You can use the employee bathroom. There are no public bathrooms," Maye explained. "I can show you where the bathroom is located."

"Please," Rhonda said and then did a little "I gotta go" dance.

"You can make the tea when you return, Maye," Mrs. Owens spoke in a stern tone.

"Oh sure, that'll be fine," Rita agreed.

"This way," Maye told Rhonda. Rhonda smiled at Rita and exited the kitchen.

Rita began clapping her hands together. "Say, this is some kitchen," she said in an impressed voice. "And look at that back door. Boy, I bet there's a good view outside."

"Sure is," Benita claimed. "The back door opens up to a back drive but beyond that...nothing but open air and the bright lights of Los Angeles."

"Really? Gosh!" Rita gushed. "Can I take a look, Mrs. Owens?"

"If you must," Mrs. Owens sighed.

Rita rushed over to the back door, disengaged a set of strong locks that were enough to keep any criminal at bay, and pulled the door open. A concrete driveway greeted her eyes but, as Benita had stated, Los Angeles lay off in the distance like a shimmering sea of lights, sounds, and buildings all joined into one giant wave.

"My goodness," Rita exclaimed, allowing her eyes to search the back for security cameras. To her delight not one single security camera was in view. Why? Rita didn't know. It seemed, at least in her mind, that security was focused on the front of the mansion. Why bother watching a kitchen door or a bunch of old people wandering around flower gardens?

"Yes...it's really a sight to see, huh?" Benita said and hurried over to Rita. "I used to eat my lunch right out there on that bench and just stare and stare down at the city."

"Get Mrs. Owens to the sitting room," Rita whispered in a quick voice and then said: "I could stand here all night."

Benita eased her eyes over to Rita. Rita shot her a "get moving" look. "Oh sure...got it," Benita whispered back and hurried back to Mrs. Owens. "Let's go back to the sitting room, Mrs. Owens."

"Oh sure, go on ahead. I'll be right behind you after I take a few photos," Rita explained and then patted her purse. Mrs. Owens studied Rita's silly face, thought of the woman as a stupid star-dazed imbecile, and then left the kitchen with Benita. Rita quickly scanned the backyard and then began to close the back door. Before she could, Charlie stepped around a stone wall and appeared before Rita's eyes. "Oh...Charlie... you spooked me."

Charlie hurried over to Rita, stuck his head into the kitchen, and then let out a little whistle. Billy and Brad came running. "Hi there." Billy beamed at Rita, excited as a schoolboy being tossed into a candy store. "Look at me, will you! Billy Northfield in the big city."

Brad eased past Billy and studied the kitchen. "Where's —" Before he could finish his sentence the cell phone in Charlie's pocket rang.

"Right there," Rita told Brad.

Charlie quickly answered Rhonda's call. "We're inside."

"You're early," Rhonda whispered, standing in a medium-size bathroom that reminded her of a hospital bathroom. Maybe the mansion was fancy and nice, but the employee bathroom sure wasn't.

"Tell Rhonda to hurry to the sitting room," Rita told Charlie.

"Get to the sitting room," Charlie ordered Rhonda, speaking in a tough voice instead of his usual pleasant voice. "I'm going for Thorn Bedford. Billy and Brad are with me. They're going to secure the back door. The back door is our exit."

"Got it," Rhonda told Charlie, feeling a strange sense of love—and confidence—for the man. Charlie was in control of the case and that was just fine with her. The old-timer knew the ropes.

Charlie put his phone away. "Rita, meet Rhonda in the sitting room and don't leave Benita."

Rita studied Charlie's eyes. The man appeared...changed. His eyes were now covered with a gray shadow that was keeping everyone at bay. The man was in his zone and wasn't going to allow anyone to distract him from his mission. "Just Thorn, right?" she asked. "We still have nothing on Ron Agatha."

"We will," Charlie assured Rita. "Now move."

Rita hesitated. What was Charlie planning? "Charlie, we have our plan set in place."

Charlie took a cheap cigar out of his pocket with a steady hand. "Rita," he said in a careful voice, "this is my city...well, it used to be." Charlie turned and threw his eyes out at the glimmering city standing off in the distance. "I've ridden these canyon roads countless times...chased crooks through alleys...fished dead bodies out of the Pacific...in the old days. But now I'm a forgotten relic, hired to chase down petty criminals or catch pickpockets. I work for a company that sees me as a crack in the floor rather than a skilled detective." Charlie kept his eyes on the shimmering city that was sitting under a bright sun. "Thorn Bedford is a big name. If I take him down, I'll bring my name out of the mud. And Ron Agatha, well, he may not be big-time anymore, but he was once. If I take him down along with Thorn Bedford, people will take notice of me again—and maybe I'll be able to stand proud for a little while longer." Charlie finally turned and looked into Rita's beautiful, concerned face. "This is my case, Rita. I have everything to gain and nothing to lose. You focus on protecting Benita. I'll get the answers and take down the big players."

Rita wasn't certain how to respond. What did she have to gain by demanding leadership in the case? Nothing. Charlie

Cook, on the other hand, had everything to gain—mostly his reputation, and in Charlie's business. reputation was everything. Without a strong reputation, a private detective had no power over his enemies and no lure to his clients. "Okay, Charlie...you're the boss."

Charlie's face formed a grateful smile. "And you're my friend," he told Rita. "Now, get back to Benita. Brad, Billy, stand outside the back door. Stay out of sight. If anyone comes through this back door that's loaded with trouble, take them down."

Brad studied Charlie's face and found an old-timer, much like himself, who needed one last ride in the saddle. "You got it, Charlie. Let's move, Billy."

Billy winked at Rita. "Your folks sure is going to get a kick out of this mule," he chuckled and hurried off with Brad.

Charlie quickly closed the back door. "Okay, Rita, let's get to work."

"Please be careful," Rita begged Charlie, and to her own shock, hugged the man. "I've become very fond of you and so has Rhonda."

"As I have you," Charlie whispered and then patted Rita's back. "Now, hurry, back into position."

Rita nodded and hurried out of the kitchen, found her way to a beautiful room adorned with a lovely, lush, blue carpet surrounded by antique bookshelves, and entered just as Rhonda appeared in a second doorway with Maye.

"Hey, just in time," Benita said and pointed at the fireplace. "I just put more wood on the fire."

Rita nodded at Rhonda in a way that told her sister Charlie was inside. "Sounds good," she said and looked at Mrs. Owens. Mrs. Owens frowned, sat down in a white sitting chair, and stared at the fireplace.

"I do wish to be alone with you, Benita," she sighed. "I was wishing to talk to you about an important matter."

"I'll go work on the tea," Maye told Mrs. Owen and quickly dismissed herself.

"Uh…I guess we can stand out in the hallway," Rita told Rhonda. "No sense in making a nuisance of ourselves if Mrs. Owens has something private to tell Benita."

"I guess so," Rhonda agreed, joining Rita and stepping out into a long, lavish hallway lined with artwork that actually made sense to the eyes. "Well?" she whispered.

"Charlie is inside. Billy and Brad are outside keeping watch," Rhonda whispered back. "Charlie…is after one last big chase," she explained, walking her eyes up and down the hallway. "He's going after Thorn Bedford, and I guess he'll let us play Ron Agatha out later on."

Rhonda felt a nervous knot form in her stomach. Then she remembered how Charlie had outsmarted her in Clovedale Falls. "Well, he did sneak through our roadblock."

"Charlie is a skilled detective," Rita reminded her. "He has brains."

"Then why are we both standing here worried?" Rhonda asked.

Rita looked into her sister's eyes and then made a pained face. "Because Thorn Bedford and Ron Agatha are both killers," she said. She stuck her head into the sitting room, saw Benita sit down next to Mrs. Owens, and decided to move. "Okay, let's go find Charlie."

"You bet." Rhonda grabbed Rita's hand and they began moving down the long hallway. "I feel like I'm back at the Clovedale Falls Retirement Home. All these hallways…."

Rita understood Rhonda's frustration. "This way," she said, coming to the end of the hallway and hanging a hard left. "The main foyer is this way. The personnel offices should be close by."

Rhonda followed Rita back into the main foyer and slid to a stop. Three different hallways branched off in three different directions. "Okay…kitchen…that way. Ron Agatha walked off down that hallway. Who knows where that hallway leads."

"We follow the hallway Ron used," Rita said in an urgent voice and took off running.

As Rita and Rhonda began making their way toward Ron's office, Thorn was backing up with his hands raised up into the air. "What is this?" he growled at Ron. "Put that gun down, old man, before you hurt yourself."

"Oh no," Ron hissed as his eyes turned dark, "you're the one that's going to get hurt, Mr. Bedford. You see, I believe you have been lying to me. Oh yes, you have." Ron locked his office door. "You murdered Lloyd because you wanted the money all for yourself. Oh yes, I know. Only Lloyd passed off the bank codes to Benita; at least that's what you believed."

Thorn felt rage burst through his chest. So, the old man wasn't stupid. "Lloyd confessed to me that he gave Benita the bank codes, old man. The woman is going to surrender those bank codes to me too—"

"Oh, is she?" Ron asked. "Mr. Bedford, has it ever occurred to you that Lloyd lied?"

"Then why did he go to Clovedale Falls?" Thorn hissed.

"Perhaps to kill two birds with one stone?" Ron suggested. "Perhaps to kill you and then kill Benita Cayberry? Oh yes, I've considered that option recently. Lloyd wasn't a stupid man." Ron stared at Thorn. "One question I didn't ask myself was how you knew Lloyd was in Clovedale Falls. How did you find out so quickly? Out of all my worry, I neglected to ask myself that question until this very night. Worry causes a man to...have clouded thoughts sometimes."

Thorn studied the old gun Ron was holding. Old or not, the gun was still very deadly. Back in the old days a six-shooter took down a lot of people—not a fancy Glock 19, but a simple six-shooter. If Thorn tried to go for his gun, Ron would surely shoot him down. "Look, old man, we can talk about this," he said, trying to sound easy and calm. "So what if I was going for the money? We're all criminals, right? Sure we are. You're stealing money from some pretty bad people. I steal money from you…it's how the game works."

"And this is how the game is going to end," Ron assured Thorn. "Get over there, next to the closet."

Thorn shook his head. "If you're going to shoot me down, then you're going to do it where I stand."

"So be it," Ron promised and used his old trigger finger to get a clean shot off at Thorn. Thorn heard the gun explode and felt a bullet slam into his chest. Luckily, he was wearing a bulletproof vest. Still, the force of the bullet—the pain of being shot—threw him down onto the carpet. He played dead. "Goodbye, Mr. Bedford."

Charlie, who was standing right outside Ron's office door, heard the gunshot. "It's going down," he said, yanking out his own gun. He then kicked open the office door with a hard foot. "Hands in the air!" he yelled, charging into the office.

Ron spun around, spotted Charlie Cook aiming a six-shooter at him, and immediately dropped his gun. "He tried to kill me, Mr. Cook." Ron nodded his head at Thorn. "That man killed Lloyd Debkins. He confessed to me. See?" Ron slowly reached into his jacket pocket and pulled out a small black tape recorder. "I have everything on tape." Ron quickly switched the tape recorder off. It was time to kill Charlie Cook…somehow.

Charlie ordered Ron to toss the tape recorder onto his desk. Ron nodded and approached his desk. As he did, Charlie noticed Thorn's right arm slowly begin moving. The man wasn't dead. "Hands—" Before Charlie could finish his sentence Rita and Rhonda appeared in the office doorway with their guns at the ready. Instead of being upset, Charlie was glad to see his girls. He quickly motioned to Thorn. Rita and Rhonda looked down, saw Thorn's arm moving, and then looked at Charlie. "On your feet Mr. Bedford!"

"Now!" Rhonda yelled. "I have my gun trained on you!"

"What?" Ron asked in a shocked voice.

Thorn let out a miserable growl, rolled over, rubbed his chest, and then painfully crawled to his feet. "Bulletproof vest, you stupid old man!"

Charlie grinned. It was time to bag him some turkeys.

"He shot me!" Thorn yelled. "That miserable old man shot me!"

"Shut up!" Ron yelled back. "You tried to kill me!"

Thorn glared at Charlie, Rita, and Rhonda. "I should have killed you two on the road and then gone back for the old man," he hissed. "I was assuming you two were smart enough to take a warning! I was wrong!"

"You're going to prison," Rita promised Thorn and then focused on Ron. "And so are you."

"Me? For what?" Ron barked at Rita. "I haven't broken any laws, for crying out loud. Why, that man tried to murder me in my own office and—"

"Oh shut up," Thorn yelled. "Old man, don't you get it?" he asked, assuming Rita and Rhonda knew the truth. "They know all about the stolen bank codes. They know you've been stealing money from the big boys and hiding it away in a secret bank account. They know Debkins found out and stole your money." Thorn shook his head. "Benita has told the cops everything they want to know."

"Actually, Benita hasn't been too helpful," Rhonda told Thorn. "But you have. Thanks for cutting out a lot of legwork."

"That's right." Rita smiled. "My sister and I were going to try and play Mr. Agatha in order to get the truth out of him. You just saved us a lot of time."

"Why...that man is lying," Ron insisted. "I run an honest,

clean home. Why…I've never broken the law in all of my life."

"I dare to disagree," Charlie objected. He reached into his pocket, yanked out a cheap cigar, and grinned. "Ron, you're as crooked as they come. You're also going to spend the rest of your years behind bars."

Ron decided to stop playing innocent. "Prove I'm guilty," he snapped. "Go ahead, Charlie Cook, prove to a jury that Thorn Bedford is speaking the truth. Prove it!"

Charlie simply patted his coat pocket. "I already have," he said and pulled out a brown envelope. "Sorry, girls," he told Rita and Rhonda, "I've been forcing Benita to play dumb with you," he lied. "This case belongs to me." Charlie focused on Ron. "Inside this envelope are bank papers, Ron. You can guess what the papers hold, right? Sure you can. There's enough evidence in this little envelope to send you away for a long time—and make a few alley dogs angry enough to hunt you down."

Ron gulped. "It's…impossible…I mean—"

"I told you, old man," Thorn growled, "Benita talked."

Rita and Rhonda glanced at each other with confused eyes. What game was Charlie playing now? Did the man actually have damaging evidence? Had Benita been playing dumb all along?

"Talk," Rita fired at Ron, deciding to play along and ask questions later.

"Look…Thorn…he killed Lloyd…I didn't have anything to do with that." Ron began to break as he stared at the envelope Charlie was holding.

"Yeah, that's right, I killed Lloyd Debkins," Thorn snapped. "But you better understand I know some very powerful people who will have me flying free in no time."

"See," Ron said, "he even admits it. All I did…well…okay, it's true. I was laundering money for some people…and taking some for myself. Is that so bad? I was taking the money in order to buy a studio. So what if I was stealing money from criminals?"

"Names?" Charlie asked. "Give me the names of the big fish and I'll let the little fish go."

Ron studied Charlie's eyes. The man was telling the truth. "Ryan Hawkins...Shelia Alders...Richmond North... Catherine Snow. They're running a gun operation...using illegals as mules."

Charlie nodded his head. "Listen to me," he told Ron, "you have one week to sell this home and get lost. Is that clear? I don't want to see you back in Los Angeles. If I do, I'm going to let the four people you just named in on a little secret. Now get lost."

"Charlie?" Rita asked in a concerned voice.

"Let him go," Charlie ordered. "Ron, leave through the back door."

Ron licked his old lips. "Sure...yes, okay," he said and hurried out of his office.

"Cuff him," Charlie ordered Rita and Rhonda, pulling a pair of handcuffs out of his pocket. He smiled. "Don't worry, ladies, Ron will be right back."

"The envelope?" Rita asked.

Charlie's smile widened. He reached into the pocket of his trench coat again and pulled out a hidden tape recorder and turned it off. "I had a hunch," he said, winking at Rita and Rhonda, "and decided to bluff a snake."

Rita and Rhonda both smiled from ear to ear. "Okay, you, hands behind your back," Rhonda ordered Thorn. Thorn stared at the Glock 19 Rhonda was aiming at him and decided to take his revenge later. What Thorn didn't know was that he was going to be shipped back to Georgia and tried for murder by a Georgia jury—a jury who would throw Thorn on death row. The man would never see freedom again.

"Well," Rita said after Rhonda handcuffed Thorn's hands

behind his back, "you did it, Charlie. You even bluffed me. I wish you would have told me your plan—"

"I wasn't sure if I could bluff Ron," Charlie confessed. "If my plan failed, I knew I had your plan to fall back on. I knew Ron was in some serious financial trouble and you and Rhonda were great bait."

Rita smiled. "You're good."

"Well…maybe," Charlie admitted. He began humming an old Christian hymn, walking out of the office just as Benita burst in. Benita had been standing out in the hallway watching everything.

"I'm a grandchild! I mean…she's my grandmother…I mean…." Benita said, tripping all over herself. "I mean…Mrs. Owens…she told me the whole story…." Benita saw Thorn staring at her. "Oh, what are you staring at?" she asked and stuck out her tongue. "I saw Rhonda cuff you, chump. Ain't so tough now, are you…are you…huh?"

"Get lost!" Thorn yelled and made a running motion at Benita. Benita let out a frightened yelp, nearly wet herself, and took off running.

Rhonda rolled her eyes and then used the phone on Ron's desk to call the local police. Ten minutes later, Brad and Billy appeared with Ron. Brad had Ron in a pair of handcuffs. "Lose someone?" Billy asked. "Found this varmint trying to sneak away."

"We sure did." Rita smiled and then hugged Billy and kissed him. "You're mine. Who cares what my parents think?" Billy turned red as an apple and blushed all over.

"Come on, everyone out," Rhonda ordered. "Let's leave Rita and Billy alone." Rhonda grabbed Thorn's right arm and dragged him out of the office.

"Where is Charlie? Charlie said I could leave," Ron cried in a miserable voice. "Please…go find Charlie Cook."

"Shut up," Brad snapped at Ron and pulled the old man out into the hallway. "I'm not in the mood." Brad quickly locked eyes with Thorn. "I would make you eat a bullet but a Georgia jury is going to do far worse."

"Take your best shot," Thorn snapped.

Brad shoved his face into Thorn's. "Boy, you should have killed me when you had the chance," he said in a voice that actually sent fear into Thorn's heart. "Georgia has the death penalty. Remember that."

Rhonda grinned, closed the office door, and helped Brad walk Ron and Thorn outside into the darkening night.

As Rhonda and Brad walked outside, Charlie entered the sitting room, found Mrs. Owens sitting all alone, and carefully approached her. "It's over, Lilly," he said in a careful voice. "You did good."

Lilly raised her eyes. "I feel so awful for deceiving Ron. Did you let him go as you promised?"

"Yes," Charlie said. "But the people I'm with captured him. I'm afraid there's not much I can do about that." Charlie sat down next to Mrs. Owens. "Do you have the tape recorder?"

Mrs. Owns patted the pocket on the front of her dress. "After I confessed to Benita that I was her grandmother, I questioned her about Mr. Debkins. My grandchild is innocent, Mr. Cook. I suppose we'll never know why Mr. Debkins went to Georgia after Benita."

"I have a few ideas," Charlie told Mrs. Owens but decided to stop there. He looked into the fireplace and let his eyes rest on the soft flames. "This was a Los Angeles case, Mrs. Owens, that caused a small Georgia town to become involved. In a way I'm very grateful because I made four new friends. But don't worry, this case has ended in Los Angeles and will never leave here—except for Thorn Bedford, who will be charged with murder in Georgia."

"Then Benita is safe?" Mrs. Owens asked in a hopeful voice.

"Yes."

"And the home?" Mrs. Owens asked. "The money?"

"I talked with a man named Zach," Charlie explained. "The man has inherited quite a bit of money. He has agreed to buy this home and operate it—under your guidance." Charlie took the cheap cigar out of his mouth. "I told you, Mrs. Owens, our new friends are very helpful." Charlie stood up, patted Mrs. Owens on her shoulder, and walked away to meet the cops who were zooming up the canyon roads.

Rita and Billy, who had taken a few minutes to themselves, met Charlie out front. Rhonda noticed a funny smile on her sister's face. "What is it?" she asked, leaning against the hood of the black limo.

"Yeah, why are you smiling like that?" Brad asked Rita.

Charlie studied Rita's silly face and then smiled. "I think I know."

Rhonda froze and then nearly wet herself. "You did…he did…oh my goodness. Billy…."

Rita held up her left hand. "Look…," she said as tears of joy began falling from her eyes. "Look at the ring."

Rhonda ran over to Rita, leaving Ron and Thorn sitting on their knees. "Oh, Rita!" she screamed. She pulled her sister into a tight hug and began dancing.

Billy walked over to Charlie and Brad and smiled. "Well, I figured…we sure don't seem to be lacking all these murder cases lately and you can never tell what might happen. Figured it was time I got smart and put a ring on that woman's finger."

"Congratulations, Billy," Brad said. He shook Billy's hand and then smiled at Rita. "We all knew you two would end up married."

"Billy just dropped down onto one knee, pulled a diamond ring out of his overall pocket, and asked me to marry him…just like that…no warning whatsoever," Rita told Rhonda, feeling like an excited schoolgirl. "I assumed…you know...with it being Billy...we might have been in his barn near the cows or in his tractor."

"My daddy said it's best to make a woman think twice before suspecting she knows it all." Billy grinned, walked over to Rita, and took her soft hand. "I love you," he said without being embarrassed at all. "I sure don't know why you love a fella like me, but for some reason your heart is set on me, and my heart is sure set on you. I reckon with that said, we belong together."

"We sure do belong together...forever...Billy Northfield," Rita whispered as tears flowed from her eyes. "Forever...but why now? Why here?"

"Him," Billy said. He let go of Rita and bent down to face Thorn. "Boy, you shot at my gal and it's taking all the raw power I have not to kill you with my bare hands right now." Billy thumbed Thorn in his head. "My gal is alive, but you better know if you would have hurt her, I would have hung you from the tallest tree." Billy spit in Thorn's face, stood up, took Rita's hand, and walked off toward the back of the mansion.

Rhonda sighed, leaned against Charlie, and smiled. "Charlie," she said, "isn't romance grand?"

Charlie thought of his wife. "Love is grand." He smiled as the sound of sirens appeared in the distance. "Look, do old Charlie a favor and get out of sight," he told Rhonda and Brad. "I need to be alone with these two when Detective Minston arrives. We have an old score to settle, you see."

"Will you be okay?" Rhonda asked as stars began forming in the night sky.

"After I'm finished with the press, Minston will be eating dirt and I'll be back in the saddle again," Charlie promised. He kissed Rhonda on her cheek and scooted her off with Brad.

"What do you think, Brad?" Rhonda asked, walking off

toward the back of the mansion, spotting the glowing city of Los Angeles.

"I think that all those lights are very deceiving," Brad told Rhonda and pointed down at Los Angeles. "I think that crime will never die and all those bright lights do is disguise the ugliness of the world. But for now—" Brad glanced over his shoulder toward Charlie. "—an old man gets to be a hero again and that's good enough for me."

Rhonda looked back at Charlie, saw the man telling Ron to stop begging for his freedom, and smiled. "Yes, Charlie is certainly a hero. And speaking of hero, where is Benita?" Brad shrugged. Rhonda looked up at the towering mansion and figured Benita had probably run back to Mrs. Owens, her newfound grandmother. What Rhonda didn't know was that Benita had hidden herself in a broom closet, afraid to show herself because of Thorn. When the police arrived, and after Charlie put a grumpy old detective in his place and talked to the press, a search for Benita began. When the woman couldn't be located, Mrs. Owens assumed the worst and demanded a manhunt begin. Charlie had to call the cops back and a desperate hunt began. Hours later, just as the sun began to rise, Billy found Benita hiding in the tiniest broom closet he had ever seen. Benita was hard and fast asleep.

"Well, if that doesn't beat all," Billy fussed as Rita, Rhonda, Brad, and Charlie stared over his shoulders at Benita's sleeping face. "Why I ought to give her a swift kick in the rear. That gal is going to drive me insane and—"

Rita quickly put her hand over Billy's mouth, closed the broom closet door, took Billy's hand, and started to run for the front door with Rhonda and Brad on her tail. "Rhonda, call the airport. Brad, get the SUV started. Billy, just run."

Charlie folded his arms, smiled, leaned back against the broom closet door, and began to hum a Christian hymn as his friends escaped from Los Angeles—well, escaped from Benita

Cayberry. What the poor souls didn't know was that Benita Cayberry loved weddings.

"Just run!" Rita yelled at Billy. "Don't look back...she might be there."

"I'm a-running...I'm a-running!" Billy cried as he tore out of the mansion and dived into the green SUV, nearly running all over Rhonda in the process. Brad jumped into the driver's seat, brought the SUV to life, and tore out of the canyon like a man on fire, leaving a sleeping Benita Cayberry resting in a small broom closet. Oh well, that was life and another case that Rita and Rhonda Knight would write about in their diaries.

The world, in Billy's words, sure didn't make no sense, but all's well that ends well, even if no one really figured out why Lloyd Debkins traveled to Clovedale Falls—except Charlie, of course. In the lives of two retired beautiful cops, just surviving another case was enough. Surviving a trip to meet the parents of those two beautiful cops was another story altogether.

more from wendy

Alaska Cozy Mystery Series
Maple Hills Cozy Series
Sweeetfern Harbor Cozy Series
Sweet Peach Cozy Series
Sweet Shop Cozy Series
Twin Berry Bakery Series

about wendy meadows

Wendy Meadows is a USA Today bestselling author whose stories showcase women sleuths. To date, she has published dozens of books, which include her popular Sweetfern Harbor series, Sweet Peach Bakery series, and Alaska Cozy series, to name a few. She lives in the "Granite State" with her husband, two sons, two mini pigs and a lovable Labradoodle.

Join Wendy's newsletter to stay up-to-date with new releases. As a subscriber, you'll also get BLACKVINE MANOR, the complete series, for FREE!

Join Wendy's Newsletter Here
wendymeadows.com/cozy

Made in United States
Orlando, FL
05 May 2022

17561154R00089